WORTH MORE THAN RUBIES

A REGENCY HOLIDAY NOVELLA

GRACE BURROWES

GRACE BURROWES PUBLISHING

DEDICATION

To the fierce little tigers of every species

CHAPTER ONE

"Must you be so gracious to every dowager, beldame, and debutante we pass?" Tertius Dundee, eleventh Duke of Dunfallon, kept his voice down. A peer did not shout on a public walkway, particularly when he was determined to elude the notice of the ladies.

"Yes, I must," Nicholas Haddonfield, Earl of Bellefonte, replied. "My governess pounded gentlemanly deportment into my hard little head before I graced the schoolroom, and the ladies enjoy my overtures. Besides, Yuletide approaches, and the season enhances my already-abundant good cheer."

"You can afford good cheer," Dunfallon retorted. "You're married."

"And happily so, thank the Deity and my darling countess." Bellefonte tipped his hat *again* and beamed his signature smile at a pair of widows swaddled in fur muffs and wool scarves. Because his lordship stood over six and a half feet tall and sported a head of shining blond curls, his gallantry was like a beacon across Mayfair, summoning the admiring glances of any female with eyes to behold him.

"Remind me," Dunfallon said, "that the next time we meet for breakfast at the club, we arrive separately."

"Nonsense. A brisk stroll works up the appetite."

"Blast ye, Bellefonte, don't ye dare even think—"

This time, the earl made a sweeping gesture out of removing his hat before a roving band of well-dressed young ladies.

"Enjoy your shopping!" he called. "Remember that I have been a very good boy this year!"

A chorus of tittering and simpering followed from the young women, their chaperones, and the maids trailing after them. Across the street, a petite female attired in a white velvet cloak gawked at the spectacle Bellefonte created. Her older companion, sensibly attired in blue, smiled indulgently.

"What sort of fool wears a white cloak in London?" Bellefonte asked, settling his hat onto his head, then taking it off again and tipping it to the pair across the street. "The fabric will be gray before she's bought her first pair of dancing slippers."

The day was brisk but sunny. A shiver nonetheless passed over Dunfallon's nape. "That wee princess is Miss Minerva Peasegill, accompanied by her mama. Miss Peasegill turned down three proposals during the Season and two during the Little Season, to hear her mama tell it. Stop lollygagging and get on wi' ye."

"She's quite pretty," Bellefonte said, budging not one inch, "if you like the delicate porcelain look. Still, white isn't very practical. I like a practical woman. My countess, for example—"

"Move your lordly arse, Bellefonte, or s'help me, I'll... God hae mercy, they're coming this way."

Dunfallon's best hope lay in the fact that Bellefonte, being as tall as a lighthouse, would hold the ladies' attention. Dunfallon himself could steal away unseen if he moved with the purpose and stealth of a border reiver beneath a quarter moon.

The chronic congestion of London's fashionable streets prevented Miss Peasegill and her mama from charging across the thoroughfare. Dunfallon took half a moment to assess the surrounds.

If he ducked into a shop, the ladies might follow. If he simply loped off down the walkway, they would also give chase, hallooing and you-hooing like hounds on the scent.

Where was a gentlemen's club when a duke needed safety from the matrimonial press-gang?

His gaze lit on a modest two-story building tucked between a coffee shop and a milliner's. The windows displayed neither gloves, nor boots, nor fans. No porters loitered outside prepared to bear purchases home for any shoppers.

A solicitor's establishment, perhaps, or... The sign on the lamp-post swung in the chilly breeze: *W. Bart. St. Lending Library. All are welcome.*

"Excuse me," Dunfallon said. "Find another companion for breakfast, Bellefonte. Please delay the ladies as long as you can."

Bellefonte's smile became less genial and more piratical. "They'll ambush you in the churchyard, at the house parties, and at the Yuletide open houses. Mistletoe was invented by spinsters, you know."

"Or by clever bachelors, among whom I hope to number for a good many years." Dunfallon moved off with the pedestrians thronging the walkway. By the time he'd reached the lending library, Miss Peasegill's signature "Halloo! Halloo, my lord!" was ringing out behind him.

My lord, not *Your Grace*, meaning Dunfallon had avoided capture—this time.

The library, thank the blessed powers, was open. Dunfallon slipped inside with the same relief he'd felt when he'd dodged past French patrols and Spanish bandits. He remained by the doorway, a trickle of shame blending with his relief.

Miss Peasegill was merely a young lady in search of a tiara. She'd been raised with pursuit of that sole objective in mind, and now she had a handful of months left to achieve her goal. If she failed and ended up wedded to some cit's spotty son, she would be forever classed among the unfortunates who *did not take*.

Dunfallon well knew how it felt to be judged inadequate. He

considered returning to Bellefonte's side, but the sheer abundance of
books on display caught his eye. As the second ducal spare, he'd
learned to appreciate the company of books. His old tutor, MacAlpin,
believed that a boy who read widely was a boy well armed against
life's challenges.

Papa had reasoned that a boy absorbed with books was a boy who
never gave his father any trouble, which for the first sixteen years of
Dunfallon's life had been *his* sole ambition.

Windows two stories tall filled the library with light, and the air
was gently scented with leather and lemon oil. A double-sided hearth
took up the center of the main room. A fat white cat lounged on the
mantel, and a mezzanine level ringed the premises on three sides.
Book shelves lined the walls and stood in rows on the opposite side of
the hearth. The fourth side of the upper level looked to be some sort
of enclosed office, or perhaps a room for literary rarities.

A second fireplace was set against the back wall, and a pair of
older gents nodded in wing chairs before the blaze. One of them had
a lapful of knitting. The other drowsed under the open pages of a
newspaper.

The library had an air of peace and repose, precisely the sort of
refuge Dunfallon sought. Not as dark and sniffy as a gentlemen's
club, not as elegant as the ducal town house. Just right for a bachelor
seeking respite from marital doom.

A woman emerged from between two bookcases. She held a large
bound tome and was attired from head to foot in gray, save for a sprig
of prickly holly pinned to her lapel. No cap, dark hair tidily bunned
at her nape, and only the slightest of welcoming smiles.

The very best sort of woman, one who looked to have no use for
tiaras or dukes. Pretty green eyes, though, and a direct gaze.

"Good morning. I am Miss Emerald Armstrong. Welcome to
West Bartholomew Street Lending Library."

"Miss Armstrong." Dunfallon's bow would have been the envy of
Bellefonte's adoring throng. "A pleasant day to ye."

"Are you Mrs. MacInnes's nephew? If so, Mr. Dunn, you are

somewhat overdressed for the occasion. You can start on the sweeping and make up in vigor what you lack in punctuality. The children will be here at nine of the clock, and you'll want to haul up several buckets of coal before they arrive. They offer to help, you see, and then the job takes four times as long because a deal of hand-washing becomes necessary. Dirty hands and library books are a bad combination."

Her voice was precise and laced with a brisk hint of humor. She apparently looked forward to the arrival of the children, and for that alone, Dunfallon decided to do a bit of sweeping. That and the certain knowledge that Miss Peasegill would tarry on the walkway with Lord Bellefonte until spring, given half a chance.

"And where would the broom be, Miss Armstrong?"

"Come," she said, setting the book on a table. "I'll show you around, and if you have questions, you must ask. A library is a temple to the curious mind, according to my late father, and we cannot find answers if we don't ask questions."

She might have been quoting old MacAlpin. Dunfallon hung his cloak on a peg and followed the lady down a curving set of steps into a whitewashed half basement serving as a sort of parlor. The hearth along the back wall crackled with a merry blaze, and sunken windows added more light.

"The cleaning supplies are kept here," she said, opening a tall cupboard. "The coal chute is through that door. Mind you wipe your feet before you go upstairs. We send over to the chop shop for a noon-ing, and I told your aunt that we can provide you a meal in return for your labors. Nothing fancy, but one does not work at one's best without sustenance. You are free to leave after the midday meal, or you may use West Bart's as your study. I cannot promise quiet, but we do keep the place warm, and we have a Welsh Bible you can consult."

"A Welsh Bible?" Who was this Mr. Dunn, and why would he need a Welsh Bible? "Miss Armstrong, I'm afraid there's been a slight misunderstanding."

She bustled up the curving steps. "No misunderstanding. Your aunt has arranged a curate's post in Swansea for you, but you don't speak the language. If you work here on Monday, Wednesday, and Friday mornings, you may use our Welsh primers and Bible to learn something of Welsh in the afternoons. Come spring, I will not have spent the coldest months hauling coal and sweeping mud, for a pleasant change, and you will be somewhat better prepared for your first post."

"First impressions do matter," Dunfallon said, "but there really has—"

The front door swung open. "Miss Emmie! I'm here!" A dirty little boy beamed great good cheer at the librarian while letting in a gust of frigid air.

"And I'm that glad to see you, Caspar," Miss Armstrong replied. "Please do close the door and moderate your volume. You are the first to arrive, so you will choose our story."

"Who's that?" Caspar turned a hostile perusal on Dunfallon. "Ain't seen him afore. Did he remember to wipe 'em great big feet a' his?"

"Dunn—Mr. Dunn, at your service." Did one bow to a cheeky boy? Dunfallon supposed not, because nobody had bowed to him when he'd been a cheeky boy. "I'm to assist Miss Armstrong with general duties as assigned, and yes, I did most conscientiously wipe my feet."

"Ye're a dogsbody for Miss?" Caspar asked as Miss Armstrong took the boy's cap from his head. "Lucky bloke. I'll show you how to sweep the hearth if you like. I know what story I want."

Miss Armstrong slapped the cap against the nearest bookcase, sending a cloud of dust wafting across the morning sunbeams.

"You'll want one of Mr. Dingle's tales," she said. "Winter is bearing down hard, so I suspect you want the one about the hot soup and the icy bridge."

"That story makes me hungry," Caspar said, "but 'em's clever kittens, Miss Armstrong. I always like to hear the stories about the clever kittens. They're my favorites."

More children arrived, and Tertius Dane MacManus MacTavish Dundee, eleventh Duke of Dunfallon, ducked down the steps and busied himself hauling up eight buckets of coal—as much as the coal bins would hold. He then swept the library from top to bottom under Caspar's careful supervision.

Caspar abandoned him for the dusting portion of the program— thank the celestial intercessors—because the time had come for Miss Armstrong to read *The Tale of the Icy Bridge*. A dozen ill-clothed and malodorous urchins listened raptly to her rendering of the story, as did the fat white cat dozing on her lap.

As did one reluctantly fascinated duke.

"I'da skated across the creek," Mary Smith said when Emmie finished reading the story. "Found me some skates and shot across the ice afore it could break."

"I'da watched you fall in and get trapped until you drowned," Ralphie Patterson retorted. "And I woun'ta fished you out because I know better 'n to try to cross new ice."

Mary shoved him with her elbow. "You don't know nuffink, Rotten Ralph." She was small but scrappy, and her comment served to start a discussion—not an argument—of why the author had made the choices he had.

Emmie tried to gently hint at themes such as mitigating risk when risks were unavoidable, sticking together in hard times, and using ingenuity to solve problems. The clever kittens had poured hot soup from their flasks onto the rickety, icy bridge, melting patches of ice step by step and making a safe path home.

First, they had considered the riskier courses—hopping from one piece of ice to the next, spending the night in the open far from home while hoping the ice would be frozen in the morning, asking passing strangers for aid—but then they'd lit on the scheme with the hot soup and found their way back to their loving mama.

For the duration of the story, Mr. Dunn had silently wielded his broom and then a feather duster amid the shelving on the main floor. He moved quietly for such a big man, and he worked steadily. His attire would have been more appropriate for lounging away the morning at some elegant club, but his work ethic was that of an ambitious under-footman.

The children begged for a second story, and Emmie, of course, refused. She made them wait for their daily story, made them read, practice penmanship, and study simple sums. If she yielded to their clamoring for another story, the whole day would turn into an endless story hour.

Can't have that.

"You mustn't blame them for trying," Mr. Dunn said when Emmie reshelved the book. "You have a way with a tale."

"Mr. Dingle has the way with a tale," she said. "The children love his kittens, and what they love, they can learn from. Do you enjoy fiction, Mr. Dunn?"

He paused in his dusting. "As a lad, I did."

"But you're for the church now," Emmie said, bracing herself for the usual excuses. "Fiction puts fanciful notions into heads that should be filled with only pious or patriotic thoughts. Fiction is a waste of money the public can ill afford to spend on books. Fiction is the first step on the road to idleness and sloth."

"As bad as all that?" he asked. "You make a rousing yarn sound like the literary version of blue ruin."

Mr. Dunn was tall, broad-shouldered, and spoke with a soft burr that had been more in evidence when he'd first arrived. His face was not precisely handsome, but it was attractive in a rugged, blue-eyed way, as was his slightly unruly chestnut hair. His physiognomy was fierce, for all his dapper attire. Fierce and, at the moment, lit with humor.

"The situation is worse than that," Emmie said. "Writing fiction provides a few women a means of earning their own coin without scrubbing floors or having babies. When men publish, they are authors. When women publish, they are scribblers." She held up a hand, lest Dunn launch into a sermon about Eve's fall. "I blaspheme, I know, but midday approaches, and one wants to stay on schedule. Idleness, sloth, and gluttony are on the program for the afternoon."

He gestured at her with the duster. "You write stories, I'm guessing."

Drat and damnation. For one instant, Emmie was tempted to confide in him, but no. Her ambitions were her own, and they were private. Just because a fellow was capable of doing some cleaning didn't mean he could be trusted.

"I publish an advice column, another literary frolic permitted to the ladies. I do believe you have dusted West Bart's Lending to within an inch of its life. Might you pop out to the chop shop? I grow a bit peckish."

She wanted him off the premises, even temporarily. She'd expected Mrs. MacInnes's nephew to be an anemic scholar better suited to reorganizing biographies than hauling coal. One look at the specimen before her, and Emmie's heart had rejoiced.

This man could *work*, and work hard. A fine quality in any fellow, but he was also a noticing sort of person—as little Caspar could be noticing—and that was not as laudable a gift.

"Will your order at the chop shop be waiting?" he asked, brushing past Emmie and continuing to the front door.

"Soup and sandwiches," she said, following him, "and hot cider. That is the usual midday fare here. If you need something more substantial, then the pub at the corner serves a good meat pie. We have an account at both places."

How did an aspiring curate come by that lovely, piney scent? How did he afford such a fine wool coat? Perhaps Mrs. MacInnes doted on this particular nephew, though she had an army of them. Perhaps Mr. Dunn was the family black sheep, and he faced banishment to Wales for having overstepped the bounds of propriety once too often.

"Sweeping and dusting are more taxing than they look," he said, swirling a beautiful merino cloak over his shoulders, "but I will make do with the usual. What about the children?"

"They have their bread and butter, Mr. Dunn, courtesy of Lady Bellefonte's generosity. The library directors begrudge them even that. Some of the children will stay for most of the day simply because it's warm here. Others will embark on honest scholarship to pass the time. The older boys will be about their begging, lest they get a beating when they go home."

"They beg?" Clearly, Mr. Dunn disapproved of begging.

"Yuletide approaches. Folk are more generous. Caspar and his friends would be fools to pass up such an opportunity. For most of them, the options are beg, steal, or starve."

Mr. Dunn set a fine beaver hat onto his head and stood by the front door, looking as if he wanted to offer a disagreeable comment.

"Off you go," Emmie said, waving her hand. "The shop is on the corner, and they will be very busy if you wait much longer."

He withdrew a supple pair of gloves from a pocket. "I want to know about those stories you write."

"I do not write stories."

"You are spinning a fiction at this very moment, Miss Armstrong. I'm away to the North Pole."

He had his hand on the door latch, the picture of a gentlemanly pulchritude. Emmie was relieved to see him on his way—truly, she was—when he turned back to her.

"Have you been a good girl this year, Miss Armstrong?"

"A saint," she said, though what sort of question was that?

"A saint who fibs," Mr. Dunn muttered. "Perhaps there's hope for me."

With that, he was gone, leaving a soft, cedary aroma lingering in the air.

CHAPTER TWO

Lemon verbena was a scent worn by governesses and maiden aunties, but on Miss Armstrong, the fragrance was... beguiling. Dunfallon liked using the most precise and vivid prose to convey a concept, and that fanciful modifier came easily to his unfanciful mind.

Beguiling, like the hint of humor in her voice even when she scolded a naughty child, or like the understated affection in her touch with the same miscreant. What sort of stories did she write, and why was she so protective of them?

He marched through the foot traffic on the walkway, bemused by the combination of tart, sweet, and spicy that characterized both the lady and her chosen fragrance. Miss Armstrong's father had apparently been a scholar. Perhaps that explained her bookish inclinations.

Dunfallon wanted to read the stories she'd written. That was only fair, given how the morning had progressed. Would her tales, too, feature the exploits of intrepid feline youngsters, as Mr. Dingle's tales did? Or perhaps Miss Armstrong reserved her talent for plucky damsels and swashbuckling pirate captains?

When was the last time I read such an epic? Stayed up half the night on the high seas, muttering imprecations at a literary dastard?

Cheering on my heroes and wishing the story would never end? When was the last time I whiled away an hour with a tall tale as a cat purred contentedly in my lap?

"Not for years, laddie," Dunfallon muttered as he opened the chop shop door for a woman trying to keep hold of a toddler with one hand and manage a cloth sack with the other.

"Thankee, sir!" the child piped as the mother sent Dunfallon a harried smile.

Dunfallon paid for his own food rather than add to the library's account and accepted a largish box of comestibles that savored of good beef broth and fresh bread. Plain fare that nonetheless reminded him that he was hungry.

A duke wasn't often permitted to partake of plain fare, but then, dukes didn't typically spend the morning lugging buckets of coal or wielding a broom under the tutelage of an eight-year-old drill sergeant.

The box in Dunfallon's hands meant that despite his height and fine tailoring, he earned no second glances from fine ladies. Gentlemen kept their hands free, the better to assist any damsels who encountered difficulties mincing between shops.

He carried his booty past a chorus of young men yodeling some old hymn appropriate to the season. A batch of slacking apprentices no doubt, earning the odd coin with their noise.

Dunfallon was soon back at the library and dragooned into buttering slice after slice of warm bread. Miss Armstrong passed the food out, and if a patron's little paws had yet to be washed, he or she was directed to remedy the oversight before Miss surrendered the goods. The two old gents before the fire roused themselves to partake as well, and both of them subjected Dunfallon to a visual inspection.

"You ain't like no curate I ever seen," white-haired Mr. Pettibone opined, tearing off a bite of bread and stuffing it into his mouth. "Curates is young and skinny and perpetually afflicted with the horn colic."

"Met a lot of curates at sea, did you, Petty?" bald Mr. Bevins

WORTH MORE THAN RUBIES

asked, dipping his bread into his cider. His voice carried a West Indies lilt, and his dark eyes twinkled with humor.

"We had chaplains," Pettibone replied, gesturing with his bread, "same as you did in the artillery. Chaplains be like curates."

An argument ensued of much greater vigor than the subject warranted, which—judging from Miss Armstrong's smile—was the usual case with Petty and Bevins when they weren't napping.

"Come have your soup, Mr. Dunn," she said, "before it grows cold. Hot food tastes better in chipper weather, don't you think?"

"Compared to the Trossachs this time of year, London is balmy, or so every loyal Scotsman would have you believe."

"Then I would like to see the Trossachs in winter. I usually take my meal upstairs. On the occasion of your first day with us, you are welcome to join me."

Meaning on subsequent days, Dunfallon's company would not be needed. The sheer novelty of a limited welcome was refreshing—or something. That a librarian's vocabulary included a pronoun akin to the royal *we* also caught Dunfallon's ear.

"Upstairs with *us*, then." He accepted a tray from Miss Armstrong, then paused at the foot of the steps when the boy Caspar caught his eye.

The lad wasn't merely skinny, he was gaunt, and London's weather was far from balmy. Dunfallon passed over a sandwich, put a finger to his lips, and followed Miss Armstrong to the mezzanine.

She led him into the little room he'd supposed was secure storage for valuable books.

And perhaps it was. The back wall consisted of shelves crammed with venerable tomes, while the outer wall featured a pair of French doors that let in what light was to be had at midday. A well-stuffed sofa lined the inside wall, a low table before it and a worn green quilt draped over the back.

The parlor stove next to the French doors made the space cozy, and a battered desk in the corner suggested pretensions to office functions.

"I nap here when I'm supposed to be penning overdue notices," Miss Armstrong said. "You are sworn to secrecy."

"You should have had me bring some coal up." Dunfallon set the tray on the table. "I've never done so much hauling and portering in my life as I have in this one morning." And he'd never realized that so simple a thing as keeping his hands free—for balance on icy walkways, for defense, to thwart ambitious pick-pockets—was a privilege.

"You'll step and fetch aplenty as a curate," Miss Armstrong observed, taking a seat on the sofa unassisted. "If your congregation is small, the elders and committeemen will work you half to death."

As a duke's extra spare, Dunfallon had expected to join the diplo-matic ranks, though the church had also been a possibility, and he'd thus been appropriately educated. For him, though, there would have been no mending walls, repairing roofs, or carrying parcels for the spinster aunties on market day.

He would have been groomed for a bishopric or the deanship of a cathedral, God help him.

"I lack a true vocation," he said, "though I seem to be managing the stepping and fetching adequately. Might I sit?"

"Please. We don't stand on ceremony at West Bart's. If you wait for me to invite you to sit, and I wait for you to hold all the doors, we will both do a great deal of pointless standing about. Why is there only one sandwich on this tray? If I have told Caspar once, I have told him a thousand times, he must set a proper—"

"Haud yer wheesht, missy. I gave the lad my sandwich." Dunfallon lowered himself to the sofa, careful to sit a good eighteen inches from Miss Armstrong. When she'd said they did not stand on ceremony at the library, she'd spoken the truth. The door was firmly closed, and they were alone behind it, meaning Miss Armstrong could, in theory, force Dunfallon to offer for her.

Except that she never would. How Dunfallon knew this, he could not say. Something to do with the swish of her skirts as she patrolled her demesne or the relish in her voice when she spoke the villain's part of a story. Miss Armstrong did not aspire to wear a tiara, which made her quite the puzzle.

What *did* she aspire to?

"If you do not long to become a vicar," Miss Armstrong said, ladling him a bowl of steaming soup from the crock on the tray, "then what are your ambitions? You are clearly well educated, your aunt is a fixture in polite society, and you have some means." She brushed a glance over the gold pin securing his cravat.

To remain a bachelor was a petty, if sincere, aspiration. Dunfallon surprised himself by giving an older, more honest reply.

"I once upon a time longed to be a writer, but my family had no patience with that nonsense. I went for a soldier after I'd drunk my way through university, and the transition to the military wasn't as difficult as you might think. I'm at somewhat of a crossroads."

She passed him a spoon. "How fortunate you are, to be at a crossroads. Women do not find themselves at that happy location. Our paths are laid out for us—the good path, the better path, and the best path, though the wrong path also beckons. For what we are about to receive, we are exceedingly grateful."

And for the outspoken company. "Amen." Dunfallon took a taste of delicious beef barley soup.

"You doubtless think I am ridiculous for lamenting the limitations of my gender," Miss Armstrong said, serving her own portion, "but you have the requisite masculine adornments to do as you please with your life."

Did she refer to his *testicles*? "Adornments?"

"*Mister* before your name, a top hat upon your handsome head, a very fine walking stick with which to smite your foes or to attack hapless hedges if you're cup-shot. The accoutrements of your gender are many and well recognized."

"Do you dislike being female, Miss Armstrong?"

She sent him a look that conveyed something like disgust—with him. Despair, impatience, distaste?

"I am pleased enough to be female, considering the alternatives, but if you are a woman, you are to keep yourself to dull and chaste paths until you can snag the attention of some eligible man. You are to be attractive, but not flirtatious. Have interesting conversation, but no controversial opinions. Find your waltzing partner's every bleating and bloviation fascinating and his execrable dancing delightful. You are, in fact, to perfect the art of lying to a man so skillfully that he thinks himself in love with you."

When Dunfallon would have replied, she waved her spoon at him. "And if a lady is so very, very fortunate as to become some fellow's unpaid housekeeper, clerk, shopgirl, seamstress, governess, cook, gardener, or manager of same, her reward will be the duties of mistress without any of the mistress's freedoms or remuneration. Instead, it shall be her greatest joy to bring forth her children in pain and perhaps survive the ordeal the first half-dozen times or so."

Miss Armstrong held out half the remaining sandwich to him. "Would you trade your lot for mine?"

Dunfallon thought of Miss Peasegill gaily hallooing after him as if she'd spotted Reynard breaking for his covert. Had that been a deception on her part?

He would ponder that possibility later. "What of the fellow's devotion to you, Miss Armstrong? His determination to provide well for you and to raise a family with you in a home full of love and laughter? What of his loyalty when you are sickly and out of sorts, his good cheer in the face of life's vicissitudes? What of his companionship and hard work and affection?"

Now, where had that sermon come from, considering that bachelorhood loomed as the most precious jewel in Dunfallon's hoard?

Miss Armstrong picked up her half of the sandwich. "You describe marriage to a paragon, and he does not exist, Mr. Dunn. My mother died trying to give my father an heir, and when Mama was barely cold in the ground, Papa married a much younger woman. Step-mama promptly presented Papa with a healthy son, suggesting..."

She took a bite of her sandwich, though Dunfallon could finish the thought easily enough: Suggesting her dear papa's grief had been summarily eclipsed by his desire for male progeny.

"I'm sorry," Dunfallon said, though he was apologizing for what amounted to a sacred duty among aristocratic men—men with standing whose daughters did not become librarians. Such men were to perpetuate the male line at all costs, to ensure the family's wealth remained in the family.

Even families without titles needed sons to manage the land and coin—or the shop—for future generations, and in titled families... Some titled families preferred to have so many sons that they numbered them rather than named them.

"I am spoiling your appetite with my sour opinions," Miss Armstrong said. "I do apologize."

"Just the opposite." Dunfallon had finished his soup and started on his half sandwich. "You are honest and articulate, so I will do my best to return the compliment. Do you suppose men like being misled, manipulated, and viewed as prize stags to be brought down by the most skilled markswoman, who then resents her stag for indulging in one of the few true pleasures of married life—pleasures that are supposed to be shared, unless he's a complete bungler?

"Do you believe," he went on, "that a husband delights in carrying responsibility for the welfare of an entire household, despite being as frail and mortal as the next fellow? Do you suppose those bachelors you disdain never tire of the duty waltzes and duty musicales and duty escorts and duty house parties?"

He should not have mentioned that bit about shared pleasure, but Miss Armstrong looked intrigued rather than appalled.

"You raise valid questions, Mr. Dunn. I suppose debating skills are much prized among aspiring clergy." She took another bite of her sandwich. Miss Armstrong enjoyed a healthy appetite and didn't lace herself too tightly to indulge it.

"I was never aspiring clergy," Dunfallon said. "I am not exactly aspiring clergy now. I was a bookish fellow with an outspoken distrust of authority, as most true scholars are apt to be. My teachers despaired of me, but they also knew to cram my head full of the ideas of men far more astute than I could hope to be."

"Of *men*?" She might have been referring to a particularly unattractive class of insect.

"I read Mrs. Radcliffe and Mrs. Burney too. Whacking great adventures and clever social dramas. Silly sometimes, too—sideways satire—but that's part of the joy of a good story."

Miss Armstrong set down her sandwich and bestowed on Dunfallon a smile of such delighted sweetness that had she shot him in the bum with an arrow, he could not have been more astonished. When she smiled like that, Miss Armstrong barreled right past *beguiling* and galloped into the nearer reaches of *fascinating*.

The slight detachment that she carried around like a banner when executing her librarian's duties was exchanged for the pennant of the prettiest lady in the shire, the most warmhearted, intelligent, alluring, unexpected...

God have mercy, he wasn't the only one dissembling. Miss Emerald Armstrong wasn't what she appeared to be, not at all, and that pleased Dunfallon as spirited debate, hot soup, and bachelor freedoms never had.

"Which of Mrs. Burney's is your favorite?" she asked, scooting a few inches closer. "Everybody prefers *Evelina*, but where would *Pride and Prejudice* be without *Cecilia*?"

"Ah, but are we sure that *Pride and Prejudice* was written by 'a lady'?"

Miss Armstrong went off into flights, about Mrs. Burney's gift for satire being perfected by the later author into delicate irony, and the female perspective enlightening both, and on and on she held forth.

As she did so, Dunfallon added a few other descriptors to the list he was curating on Miss Armstrong's behalf. She was lovely, a general term that seldom graced his vocabulary unless his family's whisky was under discussion. She was astute, able to connect seemingly distant points of logic that were, in fact, related.

And she was—despite the spinster attire, tidy bun, and firm

command of unruly urchins—intellectually and morally passionate.

"I'm off on my rounds," she said after dining on *Waverly's* bones at length. "I must make the weekly trek returning books that were borrowed from our sister libraries and mistakenly surrendered here. You are welcome to bide in this office as long as you please. You will be back on Friday, won't you?"

Before this nooning, Dunfallon had been fashioning a polite epistle about an enjoyable morning, a regrettable if puzzling misunderstanding, and best wishes for the library—along with a bank draft. Dukes were much given to conveying their parting sentiments with bank drafts.

Besides, he had much to see to. December always meant a mountain of reports from the stewards, debts to settle, charities to fund, and family correspondence on top of the usual mountain of business mail, in addition to social obligations that featured various strengths of bad punch.

The clerks and under-stewards were in particular want of supervision in December, to say nothing of the household staff, who'd spend the month sampling recipes for wassail left to their own devices.

And yet, where parting sentiments should have resided, Dunfallon instead felt a nagging reluctance to leave. Miss Armstrong also had much to see to—a building to look after, children underfoot, thousands of books to keep track of. Who assisted her with any of it?

He'd spied an oil can in the cupboard downstairs, and any number of hinges, hasps, and door latches on the premises would benefit from its use. She needed at least two spare buckets of coal for her parlor stove, and this office could use a thorough dusting too.

"What is on the agenda for Friday?" he asked. The deadly sin of lust—for books, of course—came to mind.

"After our story, the children and I will decorate the library for the holidays. We'll hang cloved oranges in the windows, though I daresay we'll eat some oranges as well. We'll put up wreaths and greenery outside and wrap red ribbon on the banisters. The pensioners will help, too, of course, but I'd hate to ask them to climb the ladders. The smaller children will make snowflakes of old paper, and we hang those in the windows too."

How dreadfully... appealing. The library would be full of mayhem and fun, the opposite of a gentlemen's club. At the library, nobody would be inebriated or boasting of last night's wagers and conquests. Nobody would be crying into his imported brandy about parsimonious uncles or jealous mistresses.

"I will be here Friday," Dunfallon said, getting to his feet, "and if we are through with our repast, I'll take the dishes back to the chop house."

"That would be appreciated. When I return from my rounds, I have a half-dozen overdue notices to write, and I've put them off too long as it is. I hate asking a patron to surrender a book if they are still truly enjoying it."

She rose, and Dunfallon realized he'd not only volunteered for more porter's duty, but he was being dismissed by a busy woman who thought he was some sort of clergy-in-training.

"I don't want to be a curate." He didn't much want to be a duke either.

"Then don't be." She patted his arm, much the way she might have patted Caspar's head. "What would you rather be instead?"

He owed her the truth, and yet... His Grace of Dunfallon would not be welcome back on Friday, nor permitted a private repast with the lady librarian. He would have no opportunity to lug coal up two flights of stairs for Emmie Armstrong, or to oil every hinge and lock in the library for her.

"You ask about my aspirations. I have always wanted to be a pirate king. Until Friday, Miss Armstrong, and my thanks for a delightful meal."

He bowed—catching another whiff of lemon verbena—then collected the tray and saw himself out. Maybe aspiring curates did not bow to opinionated librarians, but dukes certainly did, as did pirate kings.

"Mr. Dunn reads Mrs. Burney, and he could debate the gender of *Pride and Prejudice*'s author," Emmie said. "Not lecture me, my lady, but rather, engage in honest and good-natured *debate*."

The discussion *had* been good-natured, though Mr. Dunn's voice —a growling bass-baritone—imbued his discourse with more ferocity than the speaker likely intended.

Leah, Countess of Bellefonte, sniffed the orange in her hand, then added it to the basket on the potting table. "You do not mean to tell me that Mr. Dunn respected your opinions, Emmie? One of Nicholas's most endearing features is that he listens to me and to the children. He maintains that a smart man will also listen to his horse, and to his siblings if they deign to bestow advice. I've caught him in conversation with the pantry mouser too."

Lord and Lady Bellefonte had a horde of siblings between them, a growing brood of children, and a veritable regiment of nieces and nephews. His lordship was built on Viking proportions, and his good humor was on a scale with the rest of him. Emmie had found the earl more than once playing hide-and-seek with his children—and his countess—in this very conservatory.

"Lord Bellefonte accepts counsel from his sisters?"

"Nicholas adores his family," Lady Bellefonte replied, adding more oranges to the basket. "He and I would not be married but for a promise he made to his late father. Nicholas is an earl—that cannot be helped—but he is first and foremost the head of our family."

"And a firm advocate for the traditional kissing bough, apparently," Emmie said, eyeing a second basket brimming with greenery and topped with bunches of mistletoe.

"Oh, that, too, and never leave the gingerbread unguarded around him."

"His lordship sounds like certain small boys I know." And not like Mr. Dunn, who'd given Caspar his sandwich. A gentleman should be charitable, but that he would *notice* Caspar's hunger was unusual. Of all the boys, Caspar was the most proud and the worst at begging.

"Nicholas does not put on airs," her ladyship said, sniffing another orange, "for which—among many other traits—I treasure him." Her ladyship's smile was cat-in-the-cream-pot pleased. "Where did I...? Ah, here they are." She pried the cork off a large glass jar, sniffed, then sealed it up again and banged the cork down with her fist. "You need not look so puzzled, Emmie. Good men abound. They aren't all like Hercules Flynn."

The fragrance of cloves wafted on the humid air of the conservatory. "*Lord* Hercules," Emmie muttered. "Even when we were engaged, he did not give me leave to drop his honorific." He'd been all too happy to drop his breeches, though.

"Lord Hercules will not be at our open house, Emmie. My guest lists never include him." Her ladyship stashed the cloves among the pine boughs and mistletoe. "Nor do they include Lady Hercules."

"She and I are quite civil." Emmie collected spools of red and green ribbon from the table and added them to the basket of oranges. "More than civil, in fact. I feel sorry for her. Hercules set me aside because his present wife had the larger dowry. All of Society knows this, but worse, the lady herself knows it. I gather her family didn't allow her much choice, given that Lord Hercules's family is titled."

"And I," Lady Bellefonte said, passing over a spool of gold ribbon, "like many others, think you had a narrow escape. Lord Hercules is intemperate."

He wagered, he drank, he dueled. Standard behavior for a marquess's spare. "He has never read an entire book, not even *Tom Jones*. When he told me that—boasted of it—I knew I was making a mistake."

"Precisely." Her ladyship shook out a red and green plaid cloth and folded it over the oranges and ribbon. "Lord Hercules was wrong for you, and engagements often dissolve when finances come under discussion. All that is behind you, and this year, you must come to my open house."

Some traitorous, lonely part of Emmie wanted to attend. "That would be unwise, my lady. Lord Hercules won't impose himself on the household, but he has many friends, and some of his friends have wives and sisters. I do not care to once again be referred to as The Face That Launched a Thousand Sips."

"Lord Hercules was sipping deeply before he became engaged to you. Make no mistake about that."

"He was drunk when he asked leave to court me." Emmie had never told anybody that. Had never put into words the despair that had enveloped her when she'd realized how much fortification Hercules had indulged in before embarking on their courtship. "He smelled of cheap perfume too."

Her ladyship ceased fussing with a second plaid cloth and wrapped Emmie in a quick, fierce hug. "A very narrow escape, then. Your freedom is worth whatever petty gossip followed from his defection."

Emmie moved away, took up the second cloth, and folded it atop the greenery. "My brother has barely spoken to me since. Ambrose said if his best friend wasn't good enough for me, then I clearly had no need of a brother either."

"Oh dear. Shall I have a word with your muddle-headed sibling? You were not the one to cry off, except in the technical sense."

Lady Bellefonte meant well, but she had never encountered the stubbornness of a young man trying to don the confident air of an effective patriarch.

"Hercules insinuated that I was impossible to court, and Ambrose believed his old school chum rather than listen to me. I cannot prove what Hercules asked of me in confidence, and I have my competence." *And my books.* "Thank God I am enough of a fossil that Ambrose cannot interfere with my funds."

"You are a woman of independent means and to be envied. I am a woman with an open house that you should attend."

Why did Mr. Dingle's cozy little tales about intrepid kittens never feature a feline who dreaded Society? A young lady mouser who'd been the butt of gossip and mean toasts? One whose name had appeared in the betting books and whose only sibling refused to speak with her?

Probably because such a tale could not be turned about with a brilliant flash of ingenuity and some good luck, and Mr. Dingle's tales always ended happily.

"Say you'll come, Emmie." Lady Bellefonte made the invitation a command rather than a wheedle. Perhaps in this household, Lord Bellefonte did all the wheedling. What an odd thought.

"You can bring along this Mr. Dunn," her ladyship went on, "if an escort is the problem."

"I would rather not attend, my lady. Holiday punch can bring out the friendly overtures from the bachelors."

"And from the chaperones and footmen and even the curates. That is part of the appeal of the season, but if you fear the friendly overtures, allow me to put your worries to rest. Nicholas has invited Dunfallon, and with the duke in the room, nobody will notice you."

"*His Grace* of Dunfallon?" Some unwritten law required social pariahs to read the Society pages. West Bart's Lending subscribed to three weeklies and two dailies, and Dunfallon's name appeared in them all. If he drove out with a marquess's daughter, that was remarked. If he stood up with a duke's niece, that was observed. If a young lady and her widowed mama joined him at the opera, that was speculated upon.

How much of the duke's socializing fell under Mr. Dunn's "duty" category?

"The very one," Lady Bellefonte replied. "His Grace of Don't Fall For Him, the most eligible bachelor in the realm. The soldier-statesman, pride of Scotland, and despair of the matchmakers. He's not a bad sort, really, though his humor tends to be understated. Dunfallon is the dour Highlander, while Nicholas is Merry Olde to the life. They are nonetheless fast friends and have been for years."

Perhaps Dunfallon, for all his wealth and standing, found the holidays trying too. "His Grace doubtless needs friends. He lost two older brothers, from what I've read." The first had been given a Christian name—the same name as all the previous Dukes of Dunfallon. Kenneth, or Callum, or Camden. Something resoundingly Scottish. The spare had been Secondus and the current duke... Tertius? What a sorry lot of names to impose on baby boys.

"Those of us who need friends are often the last to accept friendly invitations," Lady Bellefonte said. "Let's enjoy a spot of tea, and I'll have the footmen take these baskets over to West Bart's. I'll do East Bart's tomorrow, though they don't seem to take their decorating as seriously as West Bart's does."

Because East Bart's did not welcome every urchin, pensioner, or stray cat through its doors. "East Bart's has a different set of patrons, but we are all devoted to reading for pleasure and improvement, and we all appreciate your support, my lady."

Emmie owed much to Lady Bellefonte, and her ladyship had never expected anything other than a well-run library in return.

"I am happy to support the libraries," she said. "Books were one of few comforts I had growing up, and all of my children are avid readers. Let us repair to a cozy sitting room, my dear. A conservatory in winter always feels a little stuffy to me, though winter is precisely when a conservatory is most useful."

Emmie allowed herself to be gently herded along to an elegant, light-filled parlor done up in blue, cream, and gold. She indulged in two cups of hot, sweet tea and an assortment of fruit tarts—why did fruit taste especially wonderful in winter?—and waited for her ladyship to renew the invitation to the open house.

That renewed invitation did not come, which was fortunate. Emmie was happy among her books, with her urchins and pensioners and the occasional bluestocking, spinster, or widow. Lady Bellefonte managed the library's directors, and that left Emmie free to run the premises.

"What is he like, this curate?" Her ladyship asked when the tray had been removed and the fire built up. "How old is he?"

Mr. Dunn was like... Scotland. Imposing, lovely, more complicated than his attractive features suggested, and more vigorous than a curate should be.

Also more expensively dressed.

More opinionated.

Taller, as exponents of generations of wealth tended to be tall.

"He is no boy," Emmie replied, because her ladyship expected an answer. "Old for a curate, but then, good posts are hard to come by these days. Well-read, articulate, not one to speak for the pleasure of hearing himself declaim. Has a luscious burr and a mind both curious and confident. Not without humor, though far from silly."

"You like him."

"I... do." Emmie's admission was laced with puzzlement. She had found Lord Hercules likable at first. He and his many friends excelled at being likable, while they insulted a lady behind her back. "Mr. Dunn is a hard worker, and he doesn't put on airs."

He also didn't fit the description of a curate in many significant particulars, and that turned Emmie's liking ever so slightly cautious.

"And he argues with you over novels and politics," Lady Bellefonte observed.

"Yes," Emmie said. "Well, no. Not argues. We debate, we discuss, we agree on some issues and differ on others. Hours after he's left the premises, I'm still pondering the points he made and thinking of the clever ripostes I should have offered him when I had the chance."

Talk wandered from there to books, to her ladyship's vast family, to recipes for punch, and by the time Emmie had returned to the library, the enormous baskets were already waiting in her office. When she unwrapped the greenery to set it out on the balcony, she found heaps more mistletoe atop the pine boughs than she recalled Lady Bellefonte packing.

Lady Bellefonte had made some sort of mistake, clearly.

Or had she? East Bart's had no use for mistletoe, though perhaps West Bart's did.

CHAPTER THREE

"Why don't the kittens ever fight?"

Young Caspar posed that question to Dunfallon after Friday's story hour had descended into bickering refereed by Miss Armstrong. Dunfallon had made sure to get the coal hauled up from the cellar before the reading had begun and had dusted the downstairs while Miss Armstrong once again regaled London's aspiring pickpockets with a tale of Mr. Dingle's four intrepid kittens.

"I'm sure the kittens aired their occasional differences, as most siblings do. Pass me that orange."

Caspar's assistance had been inflicted on Dunfallon's efforts to hang the cloved oranges. Some of the oranges resembled dyspeptic hedgehogs, with cloves mashed into them willy-nilly. A few had aspirations to symmetry. Little Mary Smith, whom Miss Armstrong had described as a reluctant reader, had taken the better part of an hour to carefully adorn her orange, and all the while, Dunfallon suspected she'd rather have been eating it.

Caspar tossed him the orange. "I don't mean, why don't the kittens spat and tiff? I mean, why don't they fight, like when that mean man put 'em in a sack? They should have clawed his face off and bit his fingers and pissed on his shoes." Caspar took a few swipes at the air, his hands hooked like claws. He hissed for good measure and—perhaps the boy had thespian capabilities—backed up to the nearest bookshelf and wiggled his skinny backside, tomcat-fashion.

Dunfallon tied off the orange and tried not to laugh. "Often, fighting makes a situation worse. The fellow who tried to kidnap the kittens might have taken to hurling rocks at them as they fled if they'd chosen your tactics. Another orange, please."

Caspar tossed over another specimen, this one still a bit green on one side. The best of the lot had been reserved for snacks later in the morning.

"I tried to cover the green bits with ribbon, but the ribbon kept sliding around."

Dunfallon came down the ladder, an awkward undertaking while holding an orange. "We can do some rearranging," he said, pushing the ribbon one direction, pinning it with cloves, and hiding the unripe area. "Is that better?"

"Now it's lopsided. You didn't move the ribbon on t'other side."

"My tutor claimed the artistic temperament abhors compromise."

More fiddling ensued, with Caspar providing detailed directions and the occasional insult—"Don't you know nuffink?"—as Dunfallon attempted to obey his commanding officer. When Miss Armstrong came by on an inspection tour, Caspar was pressed against Dunfallon's arm, holding forth about the orange having to hang straight, while Dunfallon attempted to fashion a bow out of the dangling ribbon.

"Are we having a council of war?" she asked.

"We are," Dunfallon replied as Caspar straightened. "We've been battling crooked, unripe fruit unfit for holiday duty. This specimen," —he held up Caspar's orange—"has been brought to rights, but it was a very near thing."

"The results are lovely," Miss Armstrong said. "Let's hang it on my office door."

"That un's mine." Caspar had acquired the swagger of a royal herald.

"I suspected it was. Tie some gold ribbon around the bow and fasten your magnificent orange to my door latch, would you?"

Caspar snatched the fruit from Dunfallon with the skill of a cutpurse and was off across the library.

Dunfallon watched him go, a pang of something like sadness accompanying the boy's departure.

"Caspar asked why Mr. Dingle's kittens never fight their way out of difficulties," Dunfallon said. "I hadn't much of an answer for him. He's so damned skinny under those too-big clothes. If he weren't a fighter, he'd probably be dead."

"Mr. Dingle must be an interesting character." Miss Armstrong took up a perch on a lower rung of the ladder. "His stories are so... The children are inspired by them. That Caspar would put the query to you—about solving his problems with his fists—shows that the boy has been rethinking some assumptions."

What a picture she made, at her ease against the ladder, the morning sun catching the glints of gold ribbon on the oranges hung in the window above her, and the fresh scent of cloves warming the old library.

"Did Mr. Dingle do the boy any favors by throwing into a questionable light the tactics that have served the lad so well?" Dunfallon asked.

"Yes." Miss Armstrong was off her ladder and marching toward him, skirts swishing. "Yes, he did, and I wish dear old Mr. Dingle would come out of retirement and write more stories, though I suspect Dingle is a missus. The kittens found their way home because they stuck together and used their heads. Hammerhead—the supposedly slow one—had the strength and courage to climb the trees and look for landmarks. Jewel, who loves books, remembered which landmarks were near home from the maps their mama had shown her."

Miss Armstrong picked up an orange and hefted it as if warming up for a rousing game of cricket.

"When,"—she shook the orange at him—"is cooperation in the face of troubles a bad idea? The children often leave here in pairs and trios since we started reading Mr. Dingle's collection. They are safer that way. Some of them aspire to writing stories of their own, and thus they are paying better attention to their reading lessons. Mary hasn't exactly developed the vocabulary of a barrister, but she has learned to write her name."

Miss Armstrong finished this tirade standing barely six inches from the toes of Dunfallon's boots. Lemon verbena begged to be sniffed at closer range even than that. Dunfallon instead plucked the orange from her, bent down, and spoke softly.

"Wellington tried cooperating with the Spanish loyalists, and the Spanish Bonapartists laughed all the way to the safety of the hills. Some Scots tried cooperating with the English, and all that did was cost the rest of us our Parliament, our dignity, and the right to farm our ancestral lands. Cooperation can be a very bad idea indeed." He'd taken some rhetorical license with history and hoped she'd correct him.

Miss Armstrong brushed at a streak of dust on his sleeve. "One must choose collaborators carefully. Perhaps Mr. Dingle should have included that caveat. Did you serve in Spain?"

Dunfallon had the oddest urge to hold still, like a cat who, having once been petted, refuses to budge until all hope of another caress is lost.

"Aye, I served, if you can call mud, death, gore, and bad rations serving."

"I did wonder why you're still a curate," she said, backing up a step. "They tend to be youngish. The oranges look very nice."

Dunfallon hung the last orange from the window latch, which upset the careful symmetry of Caspar's design. "I'm oldish?"

"You are not a boy, just as I am not a girl." Miss Armstrong took to studying plain fruit decorated for the holidays. "I rather like that you aren't a boy."

"You like ordering me around." And Dunfallon, oddly enough, enjoyed doing her bidding. He'd been distracted as he'd plowed through yesterday's ream of correspondence, wondering how Miss Armstrong was managing at the library without a ducal dogsbody to step and fetch for her.

"Oh, I *adore* ordering you about," she said. "You take on your tasks as if they matter."

Those tasks mattered to him because they mattered to her. "Miss Armstrong, you will put me to the blush."

"As if one could. We have need of the ladder elsewhere."

Something about that request brought out a subtle diffidence in the usually forthright Miss Armstrong. "You are ready to hang the mistletoe. If you think I will permit you to climb this ladder when I am on hand to be ordered about, you are very much mistaken."

"Mr. Bevins and Mr. Pettibone are happy to assist."

"They will be happy to argue with one another about the proper approach to climbing a ladder, where the damned stuff should hang, how the bow should be tied on each bundle, and how one properly holds a ladder still. They will ignore your advice, while I will heed it to the letter." Dunfallon hefted the ladder and gestured with one hand. "Lay on, Macduff."

Miss Armstrong led the way. "'And damned be him that first cries, "Hold, enough!"' Are we fighting to the death over some greenery, Mr. Dunn?"

"Of course not. We will cooperate to see the job done, miss, as any self-respecting pair of kittens would."

Her shoulders twitched as she wound her way between bookshelves. "You are not a kitten, Mr. Dunn."

"Glad you noticed, Miss Armstrong." Dunfallon smiled at her resolute and retreating form, even as part of him had embarked on a mental lecture straight out of old MacAlpin's vast repertoire: *Laddie, what the hell are ye aboot?*

While Dunfallon pondered the answer, he set up the ladder by the front door. Pettibone and Bevins launched into their opening salvos, and little Mary Smith dragged a chair in the direction of the grandfather clock beneath the mezzanine.

Miss Armstrong uncovered a basket overflowing with mistletoe. "I left the pine swags on my balcony. We can hang them outside when Mr. Dunn joins us again on Monday." She shot him the merest hint of a questioning glance.

"Wild unicorns couldn't keep me away, Miss Armstrong."

She selected a kissing bough from among the pile in the basket. "We'll hang the mistletoe, and then Mr. Dunn can fetch the nooning. Perhaps, Mr. Pettibone and Mr. Bevins, you might take turns holding the ladder?"

If Dunfallon waited for the combatants to sort out who held the ladder first, he would be fetching the nooning on Doomsday Eve.

"Perhaps Mr. Bevins might investigate what the fair Mary is attempting to do to the hands of the grandfather clock," Dunfallon said. "My guess is, she's famished for an orange and moving the minute hand ahead accordingly."

"She don't have the clock key," Bevins said. "Miss keeps the key in the office."

"The girl might have a penknife," Pettibone retorted. "A pick or two, a hairpin. Them old clocks ain't the vault at the Bank o' England."

"You two had best go see," Miss Armstrong said. "That grandfather clock was donated by Mrs. Oldbach, and I wouldn't want it to come to any harm."

Both old men shuffled off, and Dunfallon appropriated Miss Armstrong's beribboned bundle of leaves and white berries. "Where shall I hang this? Speak now or forever hold your mistletoe."

"Below Dr. Johnson's portrait," Miss Armstrong said, "and another below His Majesty's."

Miss Armstrong brought strategy to her deployment of mistletoe. By hanging the bundles from the mezzanine, she ringed the library with festive greenery and also made avoiding unwanted encounters easy.

"We have several boughs left," Dunfallon said. "Shall we add a few bunches to the usual locations?"

"I don't care for mistletoe ambushes," Miss Armstrong said. "If we hang it from the chandelier in the foyer, or over the reading chairs, somebody could be taken by surprise."

Somebody had ambushed *her*, apparently, and a few of Dunfallon's more wayward thoughts slunk off to the far corners of his imagination to be replaced by distaste. Mistletoe was a bit of holiday silliness, not an excuse to impose advances on the unwilling.

"I can offer the extra to the chop shop," he said, "and they can share with their patrons."

"A good suggestion, and it must be getting time for our nooning, though I haven't heard the clock chime." Miss Armstrong looked askance in the direction of the grandfather clock. "Perhaps it needs winding."

"I suspect it needs repairing. I saw Ralph Patterson pushing the hands forward earlier, and he probably broke the mechanism. Mary might have been thinking to fix what Ralph put wrong. According to that clock, it's still a quarter past ten."

"And Ralphie is nowhere to be seen," Miss Armstrong said. "I fear you are right, and if we don't pick up our order at the chop shop on time, they will sell it to other customers."

Dunfallon passed her his pocket watch. "It's barely past noon. I'll have a look at the clock when I get back. Keep hold of my timepiece for now and see what has detained Caspar abovestairs."

She flipped open his watch—Uncle Quintus had given it to him upon the occasion of his departure for university—and pretended to puzzle over the inscription. "I do believe you are attempting to order me about, Mr. Dunn."

"The lad's probably fallen asleep on your sofa, but he might also have found a book to interest him. I'd be curious to know which volume could hold his fancy."

That lure was too much for Miss Armstrong to refuse. She snapped the watch closed and bustled off. Dunfallon grabbed his cloak and the basket holding the remaining bunches of mistletoe. He earned the merriest of smiles from passersby on his way to the chop shop, and before he'd arrived, he had an answer to the question that had plagued him earlier.

Laddie, what the hell are ye about?

"I'm falling in love," he muttered, handing a few mistletoe bouquets to a flower girl on the corner. "I'm finally falling in love."

"Two inches t' the right," Bevins called from the left side of the ladder.

"To the left," Petty retorted from the other side. "Are ye blind as well as deef, old Bevvy?"

Mr. Dunn left the pine wreath right where he'd tied it and came down the ladder. "Miss Armstrong says the wreath goes where I hung it, and there it shall stay. I daresay if you gentlemen had the benefit of her central vantage point, and not slightly to either side, you'd agree with me."

Emmie watched two old soldiers decide whether to continue the skirmish or accept the dignified retreat Mr. Dunn had offered them.

"Mr. Dunn is correct," she said. "If we stand off to the side, our perspective is different than if we're standing at the center of a view. Shall we see what mayhem the children have wrought while we've been hanging our greenery?"

In point of fact, Mr. Dunn had done the hanging of the greenery, while Emmie had watched him and wondered how so mundane a task, when done competently, could be so attractive. He'd scampered up and down the ladder, sometimes holding string or twine between his teeth. He'd draped the swagging with perfect symmetry and had known exactly where a dash of red or gold ribbon should go.

And—wonders abide!—he'd heeded Emmie's suggestion to hang a

double length of swagging over the main door. The library had never
looked so festive, and Emmie had never felt so muddled.

"I'm for a warm fire," Mr. Dunn said, hefting the ladder before
custody of same could also provoke debate. "Unless somebody reads
those hooligans a story, rebellion and more clock tampering are
bound to ensue."

Bevins squinted up at the largest wreath, which hung precisely at
the center of the pine roping gracing the library's façade. "Ralphie
apologized about the clock. He didn't mean any harm."

"The little varmint busted an auntie-cue," Petty retorted. "If
Dunn hadn't a-knowed how to tinker it back into service, Mrs. O
woulda had the lad walk the plank."

"No, she would not," Mr. Dunn replied, his burr acquiring a hint
of a growl, "because nobody would peach on our Ralph unless the
tattletale wanted to answer to me and to Miss Armstrong, who will
soon begin shivering due to our lack of gallantry. Besides, Ralph
assisted me with the repairs, so he has atoned for his misplaced
curiosity. Further recriminations would only injure the lad's
dignity."

Emmie could imagine that voice castigating the Regent for his
financial excesses, or preaching forgiveness to the Archbishop of
Canterbury. One did not ignore such a voice, nor the message it
conveyed.

She was soon heating the pot of cider over the fire, while the children were assembling on the sofas and chairs nearest the hearth.

"You might toss in a bit of this." Mr. Dunn withdrew a corked
glass jar from his pocket.

Emmie took a whiff. "Mulling spices. These come dear, Mr.
Dunn."

"Because they are potent. A pinch or two will liven up the brew,
and spices lose their pungency if they're not used."

The scent was delicious, evoking every sweet, warm, wonderful
holiday memory from Emmie's childhood. "A pinch or two."

He took the bottle from her, upended about a quarter of the

contents into his palm, rubbed his hands together, then dumped the spices into the pot of cider.

"My pinches are larger than yours," he said, while Emmie goggled at his extravagance, "in proportion to my hands. What tale will you regale us with today?"

Perhaps his heart was larger than hers. The children had never had mulled cider before—and probably never would again.

"Mr. Dingle's *The Ferocious Tigers of Hyde Park*."

Mr. Dunn lifted Aristotle down from the mantel and scratched the cat gently about the nape. "A stirring tale of noise and mischief masquerading as ingenuity. The juvenile horde will be riveted."

The cat began to purr.

"He'll get hair all over your fine coat." Burgundy today, and though his cravat lacked lace and the pin securing it was merely amber, he would still be the best dressed curate ever to rusticate in Wales.

"The better to keep me warm when the snow starts." Mr. Dunn set the cat back on the mantel with a final scratch to his shoulders. "Cats are generous like that, as are horses and dogs."

Emmie went to what was now referred to as the "orange window." The rich scent of cloves wafted from the dangling fruit, and the bright decorations contrasted starkly with the leaden sky beyond.

"I am not fond of snow," she said. "When I was a child, snow was great fun. My brother and I would go sledding, or rather, the footmen would be tasked with hauling us around on the toboggan, then sending us on a flying pass down from the orchard, before they had to drag the thing back up the hill again. I never realized that snow for most people is nothing but hard work or a day in the shop that sees no custom."

Mr. Dunn stood behind Emmie, close enough that she felt his warmth, felt his height and strength.

Won't you please hold me? The wish came from nowhere, with the power of a well-aimed blow. *Hold me and keep me warm and let me rest in your embrace.*

"A good snow can also give us an excuse to rest for a day or two," Mr. Dunn said. "To be still and at peace, reading a favorite book, playing a hand of cards with family, instead of forever racketing about from one task to the next. Snow has its charms, and unless I miss my guess, we're in for a sample of them before the day is through."

Emmie faced him, rather than stand mooning at the oranges and wishing for the impossible. "How is it you know Mr. Dingle's tales so well?"

"Nieces," he said, gaze on the portrait of the Bard that held pride of place over the dramas and comedies. "I have an older sister, and she is the mother of three young ladies, though I apply that term in its most euphemistic sense. They are half grown now—they were mere toddlers last week—and I did my avuncular duty by them."

A chant began from the children by the hearth. "Sto-ry... sto-ry... sto-ry..."

"What is your Christian name, Mr. Dunn?"

He glowered at the children, who fell silent. "My friends call me Dane."

One of those pauses ensued, where the conversation might have gone in a friendlier, even daring direction.

I would be honored, Miss Armstrong, if you'd allow me the privilege of familiar address under appropriate circumstances. In the rarefied social circles Emmie had been raised in, such a request might well presage courting aspirations.

Might I have leave to use that name on informal occasions, Mr. Dunn? In those same, stupid circles, asking such a question labeled a woman as forward, a hoyden, or—for the fortunate, beautiful, and well-dowered few—an original.

No bold overtures ensued, and Emmie was both disappointed and relieved. A fellow who seemed too good to be true was too good to be true, and Mr. Dunn was... lovely.

He was also scowling at the front door. "You have a caller."

Mrs. Oldbach, swathed in a black cape and scarf and carrying a bright red muffler, stood near the front desk. She clutched a walking stick, the head of which had been carved to resemble an eagle. She and her raptor both appeared to peruse the library with regal disdain.

"She must have heard about the clock," Emmie said, dredging up a welcoming smile. "I suspect Bevins of currying favor with her underfootmen over darts."

"That's the dreaded Mrs. Oldbach?"

"She drops in from time to time, though never to borrow a book." The children were squirming in their seats, and Caspar was glaring daggers at Mrs. Oldbach. Even Aristotle, perched on the mantel, looked displeased to see her.

Mr. Dunn bent near enough that Emmie caught his cedary scent. "I'll read the tale for the day, miss. You go charm the gorgon." He patted Emmie's shoulder—a comforting stroke—and moved over to the hearth. "Cease yer fearful din, ye heathens and hooligans, and lend me thine ears."

The children fell silent, and Mrs. Oldbach left off casting dubious glances at the mistletoe. Mr. Dunn set the storybook on the seat to the left of the fireplace, where the meager light from the windows would fall over his right shoulder.

"I'm told we're to learn about tigers in Hyde Park today, though I've never heard such a silly notion in all my life. Who is to turn pages for me?"

Emmie had never thought to use a page turner. Mary Smith—who scorned reading in all its guises—held up her hand. "I can turn yer pages, Mr. Dunn."

"And who will help serve the cider?" Every hand shot up, and Emmie realized that Mr. Dunn had engineered a display of helpful, cheerful behavior from the children for Mrs. Oldbach's benefit.

Or for Emmie's?

She hustled over to the door and greeted Mrs. Oldbach with all the warmth and jollity due any gorgon. Mrs. O, a spry, white-haired veteran of Mayfair's most ferocious whist tournaments, allowed that the library was looking *quite* festive, but of course she did not limit herself to pleasantries.

"Who is that fellow wrangling the infantry?"

"Mr. Dunn, a curate-in-training who needs a place for some quiet scholarship prior to assuming a post in Wales." Though as to that, he had yet to use the library for any scholarship at all.

Mrs. Oldbach snorted. "If he's come here for peace and quiet, he has a taste for martyrdom. Good-looking for a martyr, but then, some of 'em are. You will attend my holiday tea, of course?"

Oh, not this. Please, not this. "I've sent my regrets, I'm afraid."

"Again." Mrs. Oldbach imbued a single word with toboggan-loads of reproach. "You flit about all day here with the literary riffraff and that lot,"—she sniffed in the direction of Mr. Bevins and Mr. Pettibone—"and decline the prospect of a genteel holiday tea. Your mother would despair of you."

The cider had been distributed without a single mug spilling, and Mr. Dunn took the reading chair. He beckoned Mary, and she—the most accomplished pugilist among the younger patrons—scrambled into his lap and positively preened.

Aristotle moved three entire feet along the mantel to sit closer to Mr. Dunn.

"You have to start with 'once upon a time,'" Ralph said. "That how all Mr. Dingle's stories start, because that's what he wrote."

A chorus of "Stow it, Ralph" and "Hush, you big looby" followed in annoyed undertones.

"*The Ferocious Tigers of Hyde Park* by Mr. Christopher Dingle," Mr. Dunn began. "Dedicated to fierce little tigers of every species."

"What's 'at mean?" Caspar called. "What's a spee-she's?"

"Good question," Mr. Dunn replied, while Mary turned the page. "Save it for after the story, and that's where we'll begin our discussion."

"Now comes 'once upon a time,'" Ralph bellowed.

"So it does," Mr. Dunn said. "Thank you, Mary. Now, attend me, my geniuses and prodigies, for our story begins... 'Once upon a time, there were four little kittens. Hammerhead, Mark, Luke, and Jewel. They lived in old Londontown with their dear mama, and though they were good little kittens—or ever tried to be—their mama was forever begging them not to make...'" He paused dramatically and sent his audience a look. "'So... *much... noise.*'"

The children had joined in on those last words, and Emmie nearly forgot Mrs. Oldbach was standing at her elbow. "This is how a story should be read," she murmured. "Like a pub song or a prayer."

"And the look on your face frequently characterizes young women suffering the pangs of romance," Mrs. Oldbach retorted. "Wherever you found him, if you let that fellow disappear into the wilds of Wales, you have tarried too long on the literary battlefields, Miss Armstrong. I see my clock continues to function quite well, so perhaps rumors of vandalism here at the library were greatly exaggerated."

"I would tolerate no mischief at West Bart's Lending, ma'am. I hope you know that."

Mrs. Oldbach muttered something about the folly of the young and, with a *thump* of her walking stick, went on her way.

Emmie, by contrast, pulled up a stool between the bookshelves, took a lean against the biographies, and let herself be swept away by the ferocious tigers of Hyde Park.

CHAPTER FOUR

"I'd kiss ye awake, but this is a library rather than an enchanted castle, and I've no wish to get m' face slapped."

Miss Armstrong did not at first reply to Dunfallon's observation. She instead nuzzled a copy of Boswell's *Life of Samuel Johnson* and sighed. The field marshal, decorating authority, diplomat-in-chief, and literary ambassadress of West Bart's Lending had apparently been felled by that unstoppable force, holiday fatigue.

Dunfallon crouched down to be at eye level with her as she dozed upon her stool. "Miss Armstrong, are ye being coy?" She could not be coy if her good name depended upon it, of that he was certain.

She opened her eyes, and that smile started up again. The one that conveyed joy merely to behold a fellow, though confusion filled her gaze in the next moment.

"Mr. Dunn?"

"You fell asleep despite my most stirring rendition of Dingle's tale. The tigers of West Bart's Lending decided to let you rest. Truly we are in the season of miracles, because the little blighters whispered through the whole discussion and even thereafter when we played the map game. Your patrons know St. Giles intimately, but have little familiarity with Mayfair. Bevvy and Petty suspended bickering in honor of your slumbers too."

She blinked, she yawned, she stretched. Miss Armstrong was apparently not one of those obnoxious people who rose all cheery and full of chatter.

"Gracious. How long have I... I still have your pocket watch." She fished it from the folds of her skirt. Flipped it open and stared. "I slept for nearly *two hours*. Mr. Dunn, how could you?"

He offered her a hand, and she allowed him to assist her to her feet—another miracle. "How could I not? If you fall asleep at midday in the midst of my best rendition of tigers, then you have been deprived of sleep. Make a habit of that, and lung fever will find you, or worse."

"Where are the children?"

"I sent them home early, due to the snow, but fear not, they got their nooning." Dunfallon had ordered them proper beef pasties from the corner pub, baked potatoes from the chop shop, and shortbread from the bakery in aid of their continued good behavior—and their survival.

"Snow." Miss Armstrong went to the orange window and gazed out upon a street bathed in the icy blue shadows created by fresh snow falling as an early twilight descended. "So dreary. I worry about the children in weather like this."

"I worry about you. Do you walk home without an escort?"

"Of course. The distance is all of two streets, and I'm not some duchess to be ferried about by a coach and four."

For the hundredth time, Dunfallon's conscience bellowed at him that now would be a good moment to clear up that little misconception about his station in life. And for the hundredth time, his heart bellowed in response that Miss Emerald Armstrong would never again look upon him with that special smile, much less permit him to set foot in her kingdom.

"And if you *were* a duchess?" he asked.

She crossed to the hearth and began poking at the coals. "I'd support libraries, and look after children, and look after my duke, too, though maybe those fellows don't need much looking after."

"Suppose not." Dukes were supposed to do the looking after—of their families, the Regent, the Church, the realm, the occasional armed battalion, and—on some fine day—their duchesses.

Dunfallon had snuffed the sconces around the library, save for one by the front door and another by the main desk. Miss Armstrong was thus illuminated mostly by the fire in the hearth, and the shadows gave her features a pensive cast.

"I've been invited to a holiday open house," she said. "I'm genteel enough to make up numbers, and Lady Bellefonte is kind. Lord Belle-fonte's a good sort too. Her ladyship says His Grace of Don't Fall For Him will be there."

"I beg your pardon?" Even as he posed the question, Dunfallon knew to whom she alluded. He'd accepted Bellefonte's invitation because his lordship was like a great mayfly, buzzing persistently on the topic of Yuletide cheer and Lady Bellefonte's much-prized invitations.

"Dunfallon will be there," Miss Armstrong said. "The Scottish duke, the most eligible bachelor in the realm. Has pots of money, great good looks, *and* a Highland castle or three. Lady Bellefonte says he also has a sense of humor, though I doubt that's truly the case."

She heaped half a scoop of coal on the flames and watched the fire catch on the fresh fuel.

"Why can't a duke appreciate the occasional jest?" A jest being a very different matter from willfully deceiving a lovely woman.

"Dunfallon was the extra spare," she said. "Lost a brother to the proverbial stupid—tragic—accident and another to consumption. His Grace was sent off to Spain to participate in that protracted tragedy, and he fought at Waterloo as well. Then he was packed off to Vienna for all the conferring and waltzing. Such a lot of duty, and one wonders... I am rambling. This happens when one's imagination is allowed to flourish."

What the hell, what the bedamned *hell*, did she wonder about His Grace of Dunfallon?

"Do you *want* to go to this open house?" Dunfallon asked, taking a seat on the raised hearth.

"No, but Lady Bellefonte is a devoted library patron and a friend. I should attend."

Bloody hell. "Not if you don't wish to." It was again on the tip of his tongue to confess. *I am Dunfallon, and I would love to see you there,* when Miss Armstrong set aside the poker and sat back on a hassock.

"If a duke," she said, "who is probably lonely, overworked, too serious for his own good, and homesick for his castle, can bestir himself to attend, I ought to as well. The tattle rags suggest Dunfallon has been hounded by the matchmakers ever since he put off mourning years ago, from the ballrooms to the house parties to the Little Season. I'll be at the open house, if only to offer Dunfallon silent moral support and to guard the gingerbread from Lord Belle-fonte's predations. Lady Bellefonte doesn't mind that her husband snitches, but he's a corrupting influence on the children when they are trying especially hard to be good."

The sensible, ducal part of Dunfallon's mind wondered what all this sympathy for His Grace was in aid of, but another part—the purely masculine part who was homesick and tired and dreading the loss of his library privileges—was all too aware that he was alone, in fading light, with a woman whom he esteemed.

"Why should Dunfallon deserve your moral support?"

She exchanged a look with Aristotle, whose shining eyes gave his shadowed form a supernatural cast.

"I know what it is to be the butt of gossip, Mr. Dunn, to feel spec-ulative gazes on me everywhere and unkind whispers coming from all corners. I suspect part of the reason our officers did so well in Spain is because they'd trained not on the playing fields of Eton, but in the ballrooms and on the bridle paths of Mayfair."

"We did *so well* because Napoleon stretched his resources too thin, and the Spaniards excelled at guerrilla warfare. Then too, Wellington was effective at getting his army provisioned, and he was shrewd as hell in battle." A hard rain the night before Waterloo had also worked in Wellington's favor, and against the French trying to charge uphill across a sodden field.

"You do not express yourself as a curate, Mr. Dunn."

"I'm not a curate."

"Not yet, but I do wonder if you kiss like one."

Thoughts of confession guttered like a candle in a stiff breeze of astonishment. "I beg your pardon?"

"Earlier, you said you considered waking me with a kiss—I did not dream that. But you declined to avail yourself of the opportunity."

The fire was warm at Dunfallon's back, and outside, darkness was falling in earnest. The library was uncharacteristically quiet, but for the crackle of the fire and a contented rumbling from the cat on the mantel.

"I don't impose kisses on sleeping beauties. I offer them to ladies who are awake enough to appreciate and reciprocate my efforts." *There ye go again, not sounding like a curate.*

"Are you offering to kiss me, Mr. Dunn?"

"My friends call me Dane."

"My friends call me foolish. I prefer the peace and predictability of my library over getting back on the social horse, but earlier today..."

He waited while she seemed to come to some decision.

"Earlier today, I suffered the fiercest wish to be closer to you. This is doubtless more foolishness on my part."

Of all the things she might have said... "Why?"

"Why is it foolish?"

"It's not foolish, but why closer *to me*? I'm woefully blunt. In my sister's opinion, I lack patience. I am in want of social polish, and my burr is too much in evidence when I'm annoyed or amused." Or, apparently, sharing confidences with pretty librarians.

Miss Armstrong cradled his jaw against the warmth of her palm. "Whoever called you impatient hasn't seen you waiting while Mary fumbles to turn yet another page, hasn't heard you explaining to Caspar the definition of 'species,' and hasn't watched you listening when Ralph states the obvious and hopes he sounds clever. You are the soul of patience when you referee endless rounds of the map game, making certain the children begin to learn their street names. You have the social agility to manage Bevins and Petty's bickering, and your burr is perfect for rendering the growling of a tiger."

"And these attributes you perceive in me, they attract you?"

She brushed his hair back from his brow. "They do."

Between mentally begging her to repeat the caress and lecturing himself not to make a complicated situation worse, Dunfallon was blessed with an insight.

Miss Peasegill and her ilk could pursue only the Dunfallon tiara, because they had not bothered to acquaint themselves with the man who could offer it to them. They had not paid attention to the subtle effect of mood on his burr. They had not wondered if he liked animals or disdained to allow them into his domiciles. They had never inquired about his literary tastes.

To them, those aspects of the *man* were irrelevant beside the shining wealth and consequence of the *duke*.

To Emmie Armstrong, the ducal trappings probably wouldn't matter all that much even if she knew of them. This conclusion caused such a lightness in Dunfallon's heart that he knelt beside the lady's hassock and took her hand.

"Might you kiss me, Miss Armstrong?"

"Emmie. My friends call me Emmie. If I kiss you, it has nothing to do with mistletoe, Mr. Dunn."

"Dane. Please call me Dane."

"Dane."

She pressed her lips gently to his mouth, and he was lost.

In Emmie's opinion, no institution on earth matched a good library for gratification of human needs. Libraries reverenced knowledge as cathedrals reverenced spirituality. Libraries gave physical shelter to their patrons, while library books fed the imagination, the intellect, and the heart.

Emmie had been born for the library the same way some men were born for the military or the Church, though it had taken Lord Hercules's perfidy to bring that truth home to her.

A new truth came to Emmie on the scent of mulling spices and cloved oranges: She had also been born to kiss Dane.

He didn't pull her hair or nibble or mash himself against her or do any of those other obnoxious things Lord Hercules had apparently believed must attend a kiss. She tasted Dane, he tasted her back, gently, respectfully. When he slid his hands into her hair, she caught a whiff of cinnamon and nutmeg, and that brought to mind the image of those hands—strong, competent—crushing spices for the children's delectation.

His kisses, like those spices, warmed her, as did the heat of his body when he shifted closer. His arms came around her, and Emmie was enfolded in pleasure.

Such a relief, to be held, to be cherished. A burden fell away, of both loneliness and despair.

"I sometimes think," she said, rubbing her cheek against Dane's lapel, "that spinsters become eccentric because nobody touches them —some spinsters. They float through society like ghosts, with never a hug, never a cuddle, and they cling to their pets and their tipple because they begin to doubt themselves to be real."

He cradled the back of her head against his palm, the fit of his body against Emmie's a perfect delight.

"Soldiers experience the same thing. Nothing but marching, grumbling, bad rations, and fighting. No softness, no joy, unless it's the joy of killing more of the enemy than he killed of ours. The laughter is bitter, the sleep exhausted and plagued with nightmares. I suspect the enlisted men sometimes took to brawling for the reason you allude to—to assure themselves that they were real, that they still inhabited the world of trees, sky, and bruised knuckles."

Emmie adored that Dane's mind ranged over myriad topics and experiences, that his thinking roamed freely in any direction, uninhibited by prejudice or propriety.

And merciful hosts, he knew how to hold a lady. "What of curates?" she asked, closing her eyes. "Do they long for human warmth?"

He resumed kissing her, and the tenor of his addresses became more passionate, though no less respectful. He invited, he suggested, he never demanded.

And that, Emmie learned, could be frustrating when she herself was tempted to demand—that his hand travel the last few inches to settle over her breast, that he shift to the side so she might explore him more intimately, that he scoop her into his arms and carry her up to the sofa in the office, there to...

To what?

"Emmie Armstrong, ye are no spinster." He'd all but rumbled those words against her hair, his embrace preventing her from seeing his face.

"And you are no curate."

He eased back enough that she could see his smile. "And God be thanked for that mercy. I am one kiss away from importuning you for favors I have not earned, and I don't want to let you go."

"Kissing agrees with you," she said, smoothing his hair where her fingers had previously disarranged it. "You look younger, more mischievous." And more handsome.

He shifted back to sit on the raised hearth, kissed her fingers, and took hold of her hand. "While you look like every holiday gift a grown man doesn't admit he longs for, and yet, I can already see you back on the job, sorting, labeling, and arranging thoughts in your mental library."

He traced a finger down the center of her forehead, and Emmie's middle went fluttery. "I worried," she said. "I should not have."

"Worried?"

Perhaps libraries, when darkened and quiet, also took on some qualities of the confessional. "I worried that Lord Hercules tossed me aside not because my dowry was the smaller of the two on offer, but because of... me."

She leaned forward, though she couldn't quite close the space between them. Her cheeks flamed, with anger rather than humiliation.

"This lordling was in the running for your hand?" Dane asked. "And he offered for another with a larger dowry?"

She wanted to leave the tale there, which was bad enough, but this was Dane, and she owed him the rest of it.

"We were engaged, and the lawyers were working out the settlements. Engagement means..."

"That you allowed him the liberties I will spend the rest of the night dreaming of, and that you might well have conceived his child." Dane rested his forehead against Emmie's. "Go on."

Hercules hadn't even asked about the possibility of a child. "He told me we wouldn't suit and that he was setting me free, and he would graciously allow me to put it about that I'd tossed him aside."

"Meaning you took all the blame for his fickleness and greed."

"And I have been hiding at West Bart's Lending ever since. I am done with Society, with the gossip and snide whispers. I am through with all eyes latching upon me as I descend into a ballroom, knowing that everybody hopes I'll stumble."

He straightened. "You are prodigiously honest, Miss Armstrong, but was it truly that bad? The gossips favor fresh game, and even the most wicked scandals eventually become old news."

In for a penny... "My own brother thinks I abandoned his dear old school chum nearly at the altar, and Lord Hercules has not set him straight. Ambrose and I haven't spoken much since. I bide here in Town as a nominal companion to my auntie. She had no use for Lord Hercules and tells me I need to come out of self-imposed exile. I thought I'd take up traveling on the Continent in the spring, rather than face the Mayfair whirl again. Auntie can be as stubborn as Ambrose can."

She hadn't told anybody that last bit, about traveling. Not even Lady Bellefonte.

"You'd admit defeat because of one titled bungler?"

Emmie withdrew her hand from his. "He didn't merely bungle, Dane. I allowed him *liberties*. Need I provide you a map with all the quadrants labeled? Society draws certain conclusions when an engagement is broken, and those conclusions do not redound to a lady's credit."

He studied her by the flickering firelight, and in the dancing shadows, Emmie saw reflected generations of Highland warriors. Fierce, shrewd, brave, and vigorous.

"That's not the problem, is it?" he asked softly. "The problem isn't the gossip—if you were engaged to a lordling, gossip was a fact of your life before the engagement ended. The problem is, he made you doubt yourself. Doubt your desirability *and* your worth."

Emmie rose, rather than face that patient, insightful gaze.

"His lordship bragged about never reading a single book," she said, pacing before the hearth. "Then he'd rut on me, and when he was done, he'd pat my cheek and tell me that I'd learn to please him eventually and not to worry, because he was a patient man, and even a bluestocking antidote had her charms."

She came to a halt with her back to her audience. "He should have been trying to please *me*, shouldn't he? I have yet to find the library book that deals with such matters, but I'm almost sure—after kissing you—that Hercules was the bumbler, not I."

"'Bumbler' is too kind a term to describe his disregard for your feelings." Dane spoke from immediately behind Emmie. "He is an ass, meaning no disrespect to the worthy donkeys of the world. A jackanapes, a niddering poltroon." He added something harsh in Gaelic.

"What does that mean?"

"Coward."

The word—a judgment when Dane uttered it—reverberated in the library's quiet. "You think Lord Hercules is a *coward*?"

"And a sneak. If the truth had come out—that he'd tossed you aside for the greater fortune—do you believe the young lady in possession of that greater fortune would have had him?"

Emmie turned slowly. "She barely had a say in the matter. Lord Hercules is the son of a marquess. Her family wanted that connection."

"If they can look that high, then they can also afford to have a care for the young man's sense of honor. You were betrayed, Emerald Armstrong, and I can assure you, with every ounce of masculine instinct in me, nothing whatsoever is amiss with your desirability or your worth."

His burr had become very pronounced, the r's rolling, the t's acquiring knifepoints. Outside, darkness had fallen, and the snow was piling up apace.

You were betrayed. Those three words articulated a wrong Emmie hadn't been able to name, and Dane had spoken them with towering confidence in his conclusion.

"You have given me much to think about, sir." He'd also made Emmie smile, for no reason she could name. "I don't suppose you'd allow me to ravish you on the sofa in the office?"

She wanted to ravish him out of simple desire—she knew enough to put a name to those feelings—but also a little bit because of that doubt he'd mentioned. The doubt that plagued her every time she contemplated another social outing, the doubt that followed her to the churchyard, the same doubt that had her staring at her wardrobe and trying different styles for her hair.

"That sofa," Dane said, "is too short if you want to ravish me properly, and no, I will not allow you to make the attempt anyway. If and when we become more intimate, we will have a comfortable bed,

comestibles to keep up our strength between bouts of passion, and a
clear understanding of our mutual expectations."

Emmie wasn't sure what all that meant, but she did grasp that
Dane wasn't scandalized. He was... He was contemplating those
further intimacies and how they might best be enjoyed.

And he had a point.

Mr. Dunn, the supposed curate bound for Wales, had little in
common with Dane, the passionate kisser and honorable lover. The
two somehow had to be reconciled, and the hour for that exercise had
not come.

"Then I suppose your ravishment will have to wait." Emmie
patted his chest.

"As will yours."

She wanted to whoop with glee at that riposte. Instead, she kissed
his cheek. "If you'll bank the fires, I'll lock up."

"I locked up an hour ago. I will see you home before the snow
gets any deeper. I also told the children that the library was likely to
be closed tomorrow, or would at least open a couple hours late."

"Getting airs above your station, Mr. Dunn?"

He took up the poker, studied it, and aimed a wicked smile at her.
"I'm getting all manner of ideas, so please fetch your cloak, ye wee
besom, lest ye drive a poor laddie daft."

Emmie bundled up, and when Dane offered his arm on the walkway, she took it. The journey home, while short, took some effort in
snow half a foot deep. Dane passed her his walking stick, which also
made the going easier, and when she would have handed it back at
Auntie's front door, he insisted she keep it.

"I'll come by the library on Wednesday morning," he said. "You
can return it to me then, and we will sort out some more complicated
matters that I'm incapable of tackling just now."

He bowed correctly over her hand—the wretch—and then went
whistling on his way. Emmie watched him long enough to wonder
what he'd look like in a kilt, then slipped into the house.

She'd never been a *wee besom* before. She preferred it to her former status as Lord Hercules's castoff. Preferred it enormously, and she would count the hours until she and Dane could resume tackling complicated matters—or tackling each other—on Wednesday.

"What the 'ell you think you're doing, Mr. Dunn?" The voice belonged to a pint-sized wraith in a jacket too long for his height and too thin for the elements. "I seen you in the library with Miss Armstrong, and she ain't your missus, and you ain't a curate, and you'd best start explaining, or I will kick you where you don't never want to be kicked."

Caspar emerged from the shadows between two town houses, his tone bristling with banked violence even though his teeth chattered.

"Good God, lad." Dunfallon wrapped his scarf around that skinny neck, making sure to cover the boy's ears. "You are a more than decent tracker. Do you always see the lady home?"

"We take turns. I take the most turns, like when it's raining or snowing. The older boys have business to be about, and the little 'uns should stay outta the wet."

"The older boys go begging?"

Caspar took to rearranging the scarf. "Some beg."

Meaning some others got up to housebreaking, picking pockets, or worse. What was a boy to do when his options were crime, humiliation, or starvation?

"Come with me," Dunfallon said, setting off at a modest pace in deference to Caspar's shorter legs.

Caspar stayed right where he was, a dark shape against an increasingly thick curtain of gray. "I don't go nowheres wif men who got nasty ideas."

"You are safe with me, lad. Besides, if you are to properly berate me for taking liberties with Miss Armstrong, you'd best wait until your teeth stop chattering."

"Be-rate. Is that like to 'rip up at'?"

"Exactly like. Now come along, and I promise to feed you a decent supper while you castigate me. Were you waiting outside the whole time Miss Armstrong and I tarried at the library?"

"Aye. She sometimes gets to readin' after she locks up. I sneak in the coal chute if that happens because Miss Emmie can read for *hours*. Then she pikes off and I have to climb out the basement window to catch her. You shouldn't have been kissing her with the drapes open."

In point of fact, the lady had been kissing Dunfallon. "I should not have been kissing her at all."

"Because she thinks you're a curate?"

"How do you know I'm not? I have the education for it." Dunfallon asked the question out of curiosity, rather than any intent to argue. If Caspar had come to that conclusion, Emmie probably had as well.

She's Miss Armstrong to you, laddie.

"You ain't a curate because you don't talk curate-ish. Petty says a curate is allus thankin' the Lord for what can't be helped—like the weather or a key fitting the lock it was made for. You cuss in Scottish. My mum says my da was Scottish, though I never knew 'im. Bevvy says you don't walk like a curate, as if headin' off to the chop shop was some kinda crusade. You don't kiss like no curate neither."

"Your own observation, I take it."

"I got eyes, and you and Miss was goin' to town right in front of the fire. This scarf smells like Christmas."

Such longing imbued that last pronouncement. Dunfallon paused on a street corner. No wheeled traffic braved the snow and darkness, and the porch lights made only small orbs of gold in the vast gloom. London was for once still, and the quiet was profound.

Dunfallon was not about to lose sight of the boy in weather like this, but neither could he take him to the ducal residence or to his apartment at the Albany. The staff was discreet, but not *that* discreet. Then too, darling sister Amy had her spies among them.

"I'm not a curate. I'm a peer."

"A fancy lord?"

"After a fashion. Miss Armstrong has no use for peers, and an innocent mistake on her part meant I could find refuge in the library, so I allowed her error to go uncorrected."

Caspar sneezed twice and, of all things, produced a wrinkled, grubby handkerchief with which to wipe his nose.

"You're right she don't care for fancy lords, Your Toffship, and she got no use at all for liars."

"In the normal course, I'm not given to mendacity." Dunfallon chose a direction, and Caspar came along without argument.

"How you do talk, Lord Dogsbody. You thought about kissing her, and so you read us a story, and that made her think about kissing you."

"Is that how it was?" Dunfallon had read the children a story out of necessity, not because he'd been trying to impress Emmie. "She liked my storytelling?"

"She likes all Mr. Dingle's stories, and you made a proper job of the tigers. Me and the lads have used the tigers' rig to make it sound like we're a gang when it's only three of us."

"You growl and wave your tails in the undergrowth, then dash off a few paces and do the same again until the enemy thinks they're outnumbered by enormous carnivores?"

"And we use different voices, like Dingle's tiger kittens, and we sound like we're eight fellers instead of three, and that's a lot of fists and teeth and boots. I call to the others, 'Get out your knives, lads, one for each hand! Benny, keep that cudgel handy! Mack, we'll need your peashooter!' I sound like Ma when I say it, and Ma in a temper would scare Wellington hisself. Bevvy says Miss wrote those stories for us. Petty don't argue with him."

"And when Petty and Bevvy don't argue about a conclusion, it must be holy writ." Dunfallon turned another corner, and his destination came into view.

"Miss Emmie is smart enough to have written 'em stories, and Petty and Bevvy agreed you wasn't a curate."

"And they were right. I'd appreciate it if you'd allow me to choose the time and place of my confession to Miss Armstrong."

For confess, he would, and go shopping for a ring directly thereafter. One didn't allow the next Duchess of Dunfallon to pass up her tiara over a minor misunderstanding.

CHAPTER FIVE

"These are for the children," Lady Bellefonte said. "I'd thought to save them until Christmas, but with this weather, indoor entertainment seemed the better idea."

Her footman set a box of wood-framed slates on the library's reception desk. The slates were new and of the type used in schoolrooms.

"This was very kind of you," Emmie replied. "I've been requesting slates from the directors for two years, and they remind me that the library is not a select academy."

"But your library is a place of learning, my dear, and slates can be used to practice drawing, penmanship, sums, and much else that stands a child in good stead. Besides, I am giving these to the children rather than to West Bart's Lending. If the children choose to leave their slates here for safekeeping, that is none of the directors' business."

"I suppose not." They shared a conspiratorial smile that included more than a dash of determination.

The front door opened, and Emmie knew without looking who

had arrived. The very air changed when Dane was on hand, and not simply because of his luscious scent.

"You are late, Mr. Dunn," she said and ruined the scold entirely with a welcoming smile. "I have errands for you, sir. Lady Bellefonte, may I make known to you Mr. Dane Dunn, late of Perthshire, by way of the Peninsula. Mr. Dunn is on his way to a curate's post in Wales come spring."

The footman, whose job entailed hours of silence and miles of discretion, made a snorting noise.

Lady Bellefonte's dark brows rose, and Dane looked as if he were one of Mr. Dingle's kittens facing the mastiff with the cocklebur in his ear. Nowhere to run, no help in sight.

"Mr.... Dunn." Her ladyship held out a hand for him to bow over, and he complied.

"My lady, a pleasure."

A silence blossomed, with Lady Bellefonte sending Dane the sorts of looks she probably reserved for her husband when he led the children on a gingerbread-snitching raid.

"Mr. Dunn," Emmie said, "if you take the slates up to my office, then nip over to the stationer's for some ribbon, we can wrap them for the children later this morning."

Lady Bellefonte made a shooing motion with her gloved hand. "Do as you are told, *Mr. Dunn*. Run along."

He hefted the box of slates and made for the steps.

Lady Bellefonte watched him go with a gimlet eye. "Emmie, that man is no curate."

"I have suspected as much, and he's all but admitted the same. I'm hoping he'll explain himself without my having to drag it out of him."

"He had better have the best explanation in the history of explanations." Her ladyship's gaze roamed over the rows of bookshelves, the cheery hearth, and Aristotle batting gently at a low-hanging orange. "You have built something lovely here, Emmie. One could hardly see to read for all the grime on the windows before you took

West Bart's in hand. Mr. Dunn had best not be trifling with you, or my Nicholas will have a very pointed discussion with him."

"He's not trifling with me," Emmie said, "and I'm not trifling with him either."

Some of the starch went out of her ladyship's posture. "So that's the way of it? Nicholas said you simply needed time, and he's very intuitive about these things. I will see you and *Mr. Dunn* at my open house."

She swanned off, the footman in tow, though he cast a dubious glance in the direction of Emmie's office as he held the door for the countess.

Emmie's progress toward the steps was impeded by Mary, who stood on the bottom stair as if she'd taken her regular shift guarding the gates of hell.

"Will Mr. Dunn read us the story today, miss?" She imbued her words with characteristic truculence, and yet, Emmie heard the hope lurking in the child's question too.

"He is a gifted storyteller, isn't he?"

"Will he?"

"I shall ask him to. Do you happen to know where Caspar is?"

"Caspar has a proper job. A serious, proper job. He'll be a groom or maybe a footman, if he don't muck it up." She sidled around Emmie and scampered off a few paces. "I'll miss him, though he was always winning the map game. He oughtn't to do a bunk on his mates, but a proper job... Mr. Dunn found him honest work, and it pays. We're happy for him, though I'll miss him."

She went over to the window seat, picked up Aristotle, and stood gazing at the oranges with all the dignity of a miniature bereaved queen.

"I'll miss him too," Emmie said softly. She mentally added Caspar's change of circumstances to the growing heap of matters Mr. Dunn had to explain. When she reached her office, the door was closed, the better to keep in the heat, of course. Rather than knock, she sailed in and found Dane seated at her desk.

Reading her story notebook.

"What do you think you're doing?" she snapped.

He rose, looking not the least bit self-conscious. "Admiring your work. You left the notebook out on the blotter for anybody to see."

Emmie snatched up her stories and hugged them to her chest. "Then you should have realized these are rough drafts and not for public consumption."

He came around the desk, in no hurry at all, and for reasons known only to unrepentant snoops, he looked even taller and more serious than ever.

"If these are your rough drafts, then your polished work should fetch you a very tidy sum. You studied the female satirists and went them one better. I would never have thought to use the jaundiced wit of the typical adolescent to illuminate society's foibles."

Despite her dismay and upset, Emmie grasped that her writing was being complimented. "People dismiss schoolgirls one week and want to marry them off to the nearest eligible the next. Boys are supposed to be translating Caesar in May and taking up arms for England in June. In my experience, young people are very keen judges of society. Then they finish growing up and succumb to the weight of propriety. They become disappointed and..."

"Bitter?" he asked, standing close enough that Emmie could see the gold flecks in his blue eyes. "Retiring? Cautious? Circumspect?"

"They lose their innocence and make pacts with the demons of expedience." As Lord Hercules had chosen the expedient bride. Had Dane not peeked at her stories, she might have been able to leave the conversation there, but he had peeked, and she was upset, and he was most of the reason.

"Did you lie to me about your name out of expedience?" she asked.

Dane took a step back. "I assume Lady Bellefonte put you wise?"

"Why, no, she did not. You've been telling me yourself."

"Does this have to do with my diction and dress?"

"Only in part." Emmie stepped around him, slid her copybook

into the middle drawer, and closed it quite firmly. "A curate might well be a younger son of a genteel family, and unruly spares are sent off to the countryside on repairing leases all the time. You, however, failed to make use of the library's Welsh resources. Didn't sign them out, didn't even bother learning where we shelve them."

He smiled slightly. "I was too busy lugging coal and fetching soup."

"You told me on several occasions that you are not a curate, and I believed you. You also have a gold watch inscribed from 'Uncle Quint, to the best of the lot as he prepares to battle the forces of ignorance.' I assumed that was a gift given when you went off to university, and it is an exceptionally fine timepiece. "

"Too fine for a man who has taken a vow of poverty?"

"No, but too fine and too dear to you to be casually lent to a librarian, and you have yet to ask for it back." She dug the watch out of her pocket, where it had been a comforting weight, like a happy secret or the memory of a precious kiss.

"You lent me your walking stick as well," Emmie went on. "You are generous with fine things, and all that aside, I stopped by East Bart's Lending to return some books that had been erroneously left here. I spotted a new fellow at East Bart's, who was reshelving biographies. He's neither Scottish, nor charming, nor patient with the patrons—the real Mr. Dunn, I now suspect. He also apparently has little sense of direction, but when he showed up at a Bartholomew Street library, willing to work in exchange for use of their Welsh resources, they doubtless obliged him with a mountain of reshelving.

"At the time I barely noted his presence in passing, but now... This is the misunderstanding you alluded to when first we met, isn't it? This is why you were late on the first day, but never thereafter. Why Bevins and Petty watch you the way Aristotle would watch an industrious mouse. I've seen the puzzle pieces and when I put them together, I see that you cannot be some younger son in disgrace or a sartorially inclined churchman."

Though part of her had wanted him to be. Part of her had wanted those puzzle pieces to make a simple, pleasing picture with only a few minor rough edges. Another part of her had been waiting for the disappointment.

Dane ran a hand through his hair. "My old tutor warned me that effective deception was not in my gift. I did wonder what had become of the real Mr. Dunn. You kissed me without knowing my name?"

"Your name is Dane, and you are about to tell me the rest of it. Besides, I've seen you reading to the children. I know who you are."

"You could not possibly. When did you stop by East Bart's?"

"The day you showed up on my doorstep, overly fashionable and insufficiently curious about the Welsh language." Also too handsome, too robust, too much at home among a vast collection of books.

He studied her, perhaps as he'd studied battle maps in Spain—he would not have lied about that part. His gaze suggested he was noting details, cataloging facts, and developing contingency plans.

"Might we sit?" he asked.

"You will tell me why you dissembled?"

"I shall."

"And what's become of Caspar?"

He gestured to the sofa, and Emmie took a seat. "Does nothing escape your notice, Miss Armstrong?"

"At West Bart's Lending, very little. One learns to be vigilant about what matters."

He looked around the room, an office teetering between cozy and shabby. His head nearly brushed the crossbeams, and Emmie was acutely aware of his recent remark regarding the limitations of the sofa.

Dane made her an elegant bow. "Dunfallon, at your service, as in His Grace of. The first part—my title—shouldn't matter in the least, but the at-your-service part is what I hope you'll take to heart."

Emmie was very glad she was sitting down, because that was not the admission she'd been expecting. Not at all. "You're *Dunfallon*?"

"I have that honor."

"And *you* read my stories?" The *Duke of Dunfallon* had swept and dusted her library, hauled her coal, and... kissed her? The Duke of Dunfallon had tramped to the chop shop and back like some under-footman?

"I completed one tale in its entirety, and I would dearly like to read more."

Emmie absently patted the place beside her. She'd been prepared for him to be a younger son, a spare, an impecunious society bachelor with a need to avoid dunning creditors, possibly even an heir kicking his heels while trading on his expectations... but *Dunfallon?*

Gracious, merciful, everlasting, almighty kittens. Emmie mentally re-shelved some conclusions and dusted off others. The notion that a peer of the realm, a duke, a war hero, had been Caspar's pupil regarding the serious matter of how to clean out a hearth...

When the shock wore off, Emmie might find the situation humorous—provided His Grace was honest about the rest of it, because he might be a duke, but he was also far more than that.

"It's only fair that you read my stories," she said slowly, "seeing as *I've read so many of yours.*"

He dropped onto the sofa without ceremony. "Explain yourself. Please."

If nothing else had convinced her of the truth of his confessions, that note of command in his voice would have. Dane... Dunfallon, rather, was accustomed to being obeyed, but Emmie wondered if he was accustomed to being understood, much less appreciated.

All things considered, Emmie appeared to be adjusting fairly well to having a duke as her adoring swain. Dunfallon could not make the same claim for himself regarding her latest revelation.

Nobody had accused him of writing the kitten stories, and he'd stopped worrying that anybody ever would.

"You are Christopher Dingle," she said. "That was the secret I hoped you'd confide in me."

"And how did you divine that near impossibility?" He sounded as testy as old MacAlpin when the indigestion plagued him.

"In a sense, Aristotle told me." Emmie took up a green brocade pillow and fiddled with its tassels. "He will tolerate affection from the children when they are having a low moment, but he doesn't like men. Bevvy and Petty have never been allowed to so much as pat his head. He has hissed at my brother."

She clearly approved of the cat for that rudeness. "I like animals," Dunfallon said. "That does not prove I could pen a few silly stories for children."

Emmie stroked the tassel she'd been twiddling. "I wish you could hear the difference between how I read Mr. Dingle's stories and how you read them. The children noted it at once. You didn't need Mary to keep up with the page turning, because you knew every word by heart."

Dunfallon felt the same rising anxiety he'd experienced in Spain when the sound of French war drums had grown ever closer on the day of battle.

He hadn't run then, and he wasn't about to run now. "I told you, I have nieces. I've read them Dingle's whole collection, as well as Aesop, *The Arabian Nights*, and Lamb's versions of Shakespeare."

Emmie brushed her cheek with the silky green tassel. She doubtless did not mean these idle gestures to be distracting, but they most assuredly were.

"You have Dingle memorized," she said.

"So, I hope, do you and many a tired nanny or parent."

"You did not write those stories for the nannies and parents."

Dunfallon's panic rose higher, to the acid-in-the-back-of-the-throat stage. A cold sweat would soon follow if he didn't...

Didn't what? This was *Emmie*, who loved books and children and cranky old men and wayward cats. Emmie was not Papa bound on another excoriation of his third son's myriad, egregious faults.

"The first volume of Dingle's stories went into a second printing," Emmie said, almost as if Dunfallon's world was not coming asunder with old memories and new fears. "Between the two printings, there were, of course, a few corrections—printers are not perfect. There was also one change, made apparently by the author. Nobody knows why. He changed the word 'commence' to 'begin.' The sentence loses a little of its loftiness, but being both accessible to children and a tad lofty is a hallmark of Dingle's style."

Dunfallon wanted to beat himself over the head with her pillow.

"When you read to the children," she went on, "you used the word 'commence,' found only in the rare first edition. Your publisher did not anticipate how wildly popular the stories would become, and thus the initial printing was quite modest. The second printing was much larger, and that's the one all those nannies and parents have. The first editions are largely in the hands of collectors."

Dane's late father would have thundered at her to cease her impertinence, to spare him further exhibitions of female insolence. Dane was torn between a pressing need to leap out the French doors and a yearning to hug the library cat.

In the midst of this old dread of censure, a single thought penetrated: If he asked Emmie for her discretion, she would not betray his authorship. She was not a mean, blustering duke, but rather, a woman who applied reason and compassion in equal measure.

You can trust her, laddie. The warning came not in MacAlpin's gruff baritone, but in the voice of a brother long gone to his reward.

Dunfallon took the pillow from Emmie and set it aside. "I promised my brother Secondus one thing as he gasped his last. Weak lungs, my father said. My brother expired of damned consumption, which isn't supposed to afflict ducal heirs."

"What did you promise your brother?"

"That I would not be like our father. Secondus was my friend and ally, the person who insisted that MacAlpin accompany me to Oxford. Secondus took the blame for many of my blunderings, because even Papa would not beat a consumptive, nor would he accuse his heir of lying."

She patted Dunfallon's arm. "I am so sorry."

"One does not express pity for a duke, Miss Armstrong."

Her next touch was more of a caress than a pat. "Is that what your strutting papa would have said?"

"God, yes, and then he would have treated the world to a good twenty minutes of shouted bloviations grounded solely in his conceits and fearful fancies."

Emmie rose to go to the door, and Dunfallon's heart nearly stopped beating. *Don't leave. I can try to explain. Please...*

She let in the cat and returned to the sofa, this time sitting at Dunfallon's hip. "I gather your father did not approve of your stories?"

Dunfallon was tempted to reassert his denials, to lie, strut, and paw and generally make an ass of himself before the woman he loved. That's how a proper duke would handle the situation.

From the depths of his imagination, Dunfallon heard four small feline voices reproaching him: *Use your head. Think before you act. Keep trying. Don't give up. There's always a way home.*

Though he was not an intrepid kitten, and the family seat was a distant, drafty castle full of grim memories.

Where was *home*? *Who* was home?

"Dane?" Emmie took his hand and let her head fall to his shoulder. "Please tell me the rest of your story."

Dunfallon's heart began to beat like one of those war drums. "Not much to tell."

Aristotle leaped to the sofa and sat at Dunfallon's other hip, close enough that the cat's purring was both a physical sensation and a soft hum.

"Tell me anyway."

He was helpless to decline her invitation. "My father *hated* my stories, almost as much as he hated me. My oldest brother should have been the duke—a great strapping, bonnie laddie who loved to ride to hounds, shoot, and drink. Secondus was at least handsome and witty. But Papa was left with me, a shy, gangly, bookish disappointment—a disgrace. When he found out I'd been writing for children, he had me sent to Spain, to a unit that saw a great deal of action. He admonished me to make a man of myself or die trying."

Somewhere between landing in Lisbon and surviving Waterloo, Dunfallon had figured out that one could be *a man* and still pen a few children's stories. He'd never had the satisfaction of sharing that insight with his father.

"Dane, the old duke was the disgrace, not you. Your stories are about helpless kittens winning the day—through cooperation, cleverness, and bravery. Your father apparently regarded those tales as literary treason against his mutton-headed authority and the peerage generally. The kittens are decent little souls, and those who menace them are always abusing positions of authority."

She saw without effort what Dunfallon had taken years to put together. "I sorted out that much in Spain. I also became an exemplary officer, then did my bit at Vienna, anything to avoid going back to my father's house." He would not call that dreary castle *home*, not in this context.

"And now you lead the matchmakers a dance here in London, when you aren't lugging coal for me. Who else knows that you are a brilliant author?"

"I'm not brilliant." Papa had been very clear on that point, and for the most part, Dunfallon agreed with him. "I'm a plodder, conscientious, and more than a bit stodgy."

"Shy." She hugged his arm. "And a brilliant author."

That little, affectionate squeeze did something to Dunfallon's heart. A weight slid away, a grief. "I am Christopher Dingle." The words should have felt portentous, imbued with the gravity of a long-overdue truth, but instead, they felt... comfy. True, in an unremarkable way. The same way mulling spices smelled good and a purring cat was a delight.

In this office, with Emmie tucked against one side and Aristotle purring madly on the other, to admit authorship of some children's tales was *safe*.

"Who else knows?" Emmie asked.

"MacAlpin, my old tutor. He would never betray me. Lord Belle-fonte knows. He read the stories to his oldest daughter, whose juvenile critiques helped shape the final drafts."

"How is it you entrusted the Earl of Bellefonte with this knowledge? He can be a bit frivolous."

"Flirtatious, perhaps, but don't be fooled by his charm. Nicholas is shrewd and ruthless when he has to be."

"And he is your friend. I'm glad. We all need friends who understand us and stand by us even when we aren't making much sense."

Emmie had seen what all of society had ignored: The current Duke of Dunfallon was a lonely fellow, somewhat adrift, and not at all enamored of his title.

Whose privilege was it to stand by Emmie?

"Nicholas was sent off to school without warning," Dunfallon said, "as I was. My oldest brother had just died, and my surviving brother was prone to a winter cough that lasted ten months of the year. Bellefonte had been separated from his older half-brother, and the parting left him heartbroken. Bellefonte was outlandishly tall even then, a giant among the other boys, with a heart to match. He took me under his physical and figurative wing and was no respecter of my privacy. We remained friends through university and beyond. That he liked my stories and did not laugh at them meant worlds to me."

That Emmie liked Dunfallon's kitten stories, *and liked him*, meant even more. "The countess knows of my authorship as well," he went on. "Bellefonte let the secret slip in one of their many marital moments, but he assured me her ladyship can keep a confidence."

"I haven't shown my stories to anybody," Emmie said. "I've pored over Dingle's every word, drawn diagrams of his plots, studied his sentence structures, but what I wanted most to learn from him was how to reassure the vulnerable and the overlooked that they are equal to life's challenges. You could write those stories because you know what it is to be without allies or influence. One would never think that of a ducal spare, but the truth is on the pages."

Perhaps that's why Dunfallon was determined to preserve the safety of his pseudonym—because the sad reality of life in his father's house was in those stories.

"I like Dingle's stories," he said. "They represent my riposte to all of Papa's lectures and sermons. I could never say, 'Papa, you are a selfish embarrassment...' But I could say, 'There's another way to go through life besides blustering and threatening when abusing one's authority doesn't see one's every wish satisfied.' The old man made me watch while he burned my first editions on his library hearth. I'm sure I was the picture of youthful devastation, but all the while, I knew the stories were safe."

"Because you'd had them published?"

"Because even Papa could not burn down every library in the realm. I suspect he was unwell, in heart, soul, and mind. As his family dwindled and his years advanced, he became fanatic about standards, decorum, and consequence."

Syphilis, perhaps, or the corrosive effect of meanness, drink, and loneliness.

"The children will want their story soon," Emmie said, resting her head on his shoulder. "Will you read to them?"

"With pleasure, provided I don't again find you napping with Mr. Johnson when I finish."

They remained behind the closed door with Aristotle for another half hour. Emmie laughed at Dunfallon's explanation of his initial foray into West Bart's Lending, and Dunfallon agreed to make comments on the draft of her story.

He emerged from her office a changed, happier man. He was a fellow who had only one more question to pose if his joy was to be complete.

"Before we join battle with the Vandal horde, Emmie, please say you will be my wife. I would go down on bended knee here on the mezzanine, but that would make a spectacle of what should be a precious moment."

At the top of the steps, she paused and gazed out over the library.

"I would love to be Mrs. Christopher Dingle, and I thought Dane Dunn was a very worthy fellow too. Becoming a duchess, though... even your duchess would be quite a step."

She deserved to be wooed, of course. He should not have rushed his fences with a woman who had every reason to view polite society —and marriage proposals generally—with a jaundiced eye.

He took her hand. "I would expect my duchess to be almost as devoted to libraries as she is to her duke."

"You have the right of that, sir. I'll not turn my back on West Bart's Lending simply to mince about Mayfair at your side."

"If we marry, I can promise you mincing about Mayfair will fall very low on my list of priorities." He kissed her ink-stained fingers, ready to beg if necessary. "Please say you'll have me, Emmie."

"I can still look after West Bart's Lending?"

"We can set up an endowment that will keep West Bart's, its urchins, pensioners, cats, and pickpockets in cider and sandwiches until Mary Smith is named queen of the May. I will court you before all of London, flirt with Mrs. Oldbach herself, and—"

Emmie put her fingers to his lips. "You mean it? About the endowment and about not having to flit about every Venetian break-fast, grand ball, and musicale in Town?"

Dane was more than happy to give the social whirl a rest, and Emmie had good reasons to be wary of society.

"Within the limits of my station, I promise we will socialize only selectively."

Emmie held his hand against her cheek. "Thank you. With those assurances, I can happily consent to be your wife, though I expect to wake up from a nap and find I have neglected my overdue notices while dreaming this whole conversation."

"You are not asleep, Emmie Armstrong, and you are making my dreams come true. Thank you. Clichés come to mind, effusive, paltry clichés, so I will content myself with thanking you."

Her smile was mischievous and sweet. "Is the sofa still too short?"

"It's getting longer by the minute."

"Naughty, sir. We've been spotted."

Mary was at her post at the foot of the steps, glowering doom at any who thought to put off the reading of the daily story.

"When we've dispensed with the morning's tasks," Dunfallon said, "we can discuss particulars pertinent to the immediate future. Perhaps a repast in your office will suit?"

"A repast in my office will suit nicely. And I can tell you right now that for my morning gift—after a very short courtship—I must have a new story by the estimable Mr. Dingle. If you truly seek to impress me, a new volume of stories would be even better."

She swanned down the steps and began assembling the children by the hearth, while Dunfallon remained on the mezzanine and hoped like hell that his beloved had been joking.

"Dunfallon's father was awful," Emmie said. "A martinet with no sense for his children's feelings. What sort of man *numbers* his sons?"

Leah, Lady Bellefonte, sipped her tea and marveled. For the first time in living memory, Emmie Armstrong was babbling. She had been holding forth since ensconcing herself on the love seat opposite her ladyship's perch on the sofa. The fire on the hearth in the countess's private parlor softly crackled, and flurries danced past the window, while Emmie Armstrong chattered gaily on.

And about time too.

"His given name is Tertius," she said. "The older brother was Secondus. He was consumptive and expired while Dane was in the military. Secondus held out until Dane could get leave so they at least took a proper farewell of one another. Secondus was also Dane's ally. I suppose I should refer to Dane as Dunfallon, but the children still call him Mr. Dunn, when I so want them to be able to call him Mr. Dingle."

Emmie was wearing a pretty frock for a change, in holiday red and green, and her eyes had taken on the sparkle Lady Bellefonte usually saw only when Emmie was critiquing Mr. Coleridge's poetical maunderings.

"Emmie?"

"Hmm?"

"Has His Grace declared his intentions?"

"Yes."

Nicholas had predicted as much. He'd said that if and when Dunfallon succumbed to love, he'd fall hard and not for a predictable diamond.

"Have you informed your brother?"

Emmie's sparkle dimmed, and she considered her tea. "Ambrose is in Town. I know not why. He sent a note, and my fingers nearly froze holding it, the tone was so chilly. 'I plan to spend the holidays on Humboldt Street. Please inform Aunt. Threadham.'"

"Now that is odd," Lady Bellefonte said. "He might have written to your aunt rather than to you, and by rights, a dutiful nephew should pay a holiday call on his auntie."

Emmie made a face at a cup of excellent China black. "You think he was warning me of such a visit? Or does he expect me to go down on my figurative knees, begging for his brotherly forgiveness when he's the party in the wrong?"

Her ladyship considered what she knew of brothers—she had grown up with two, Nicholas had four, and the lot of them were difficult, dear men.

"I suspect Lord Threadham wasn't clear in his mind about his own motives. He probably told himself you had a right to know his movements, that you and he might meet at some holiday function, and you are his sister after all. He would not have examined his reasoning more closely until after the letter had been posted, when it was safe to do so."

Lady Bellefonte knew Ambrose, Viscount Threadham, only in passing. That no gossip concerning the viscount had reached her ladyship spoke well of him, but perhaps both discretion and debauchery numbered among his talents.

"Ambrose was such a happy boy," Emmie said. "That he has become a grim, judgmental prig baffles and disappoints me."

"Dunfallon might understand the transformation. He's not exactly a dashing blade himself."

Emmie cut herself a slice of the gingerbread loaf that had as yet escaped predation by Nicholas or the children.

"Why do you think Ambrose wrote to me?"

"Because he misses you, and the holidays are a time to be with loved ones?"

"This gingerbread is wonderful," Emmie said, a little too brightly. "Lighter than the usual varieties."

"The recipe was developed by Nicholas's brother Max. He's something of a food chemist, and he has a blend of mulling spices that goes so perfectly with his gingerbread that the Regent ought to pay to serve it at court. Max claims pepper is the secret ingredient in both."

"If he admits it, is it a secret?"

"A family secret, then. I'll send some gingerbread to West Bart's with you. Have you and Dunfallon set a date?"

If they were wise, they'd make a start for Scotland after the first of the year and marry north of the border without any fuss—or with as little fuss as ducal nuptials could involve.

The parlor door opened, and as predictably as bees flew to blooming honeysuckle, Nicholas, Earl of Bellefonte, sauntered into the room, pointedly ignoring the offerings on the tea tray.

And still, after years of marriage, parenting, and muddling on together, Leah felt her heart leap as she beheld her golden god of a darling husband.

"Lovey mine, I did not know Miss Armstrong had graced us with a call. Miss Armstrong, you look positively radiant. Pray tell, what has put such becoming roses in your cheeks? Could it be you've had a sample of Max's gingerbread?"

"Paws *off* the gingerbread, your lordship," Lady Bellefonte snapped. "You will spoil your supper."

"A man of my generous proportions needs at least four snacks between luncheon and supper." He batted his lashes at Emmie. "Support me in my famished desperation, Miss Armstrong, or I shall faint dead away."

Emmie offered him the plate holding her half-finished slice of gingerbread. "I could not have a fainting earl on my conscience, particularly when allowing you to topple to the carpet would shake the rafters and frighten the children."

Nicholas took a bite and put the slice back on the plate. "A woman of keen understanding. I am told by a little ducal birdie that felicitations are in order."

Even for Nick, that was forward, but then, he was protective of his friends. Also of his family, his pets, his employees, and his enormous mare—Buttercup, by name.

"I have given Dunfallon permission to pay me his addresses," Emmie said, positively glowing to impart that news. "The rest of the situation requires further discussion."

Nick helped himself to the rest of Emmie's gingerbread, for which Lady Bellefonte would remonstrate with him in private and at length. Her sternest scolds would probably result in his lordship resorting to some kissing. Not the most desperate tactic in his marital arsenal, but lamentably effective when a wife was trying to be dignified and imposing.

"If Dunfallon should for any reason vex you in the course of this courtship," Nick said, looking for once serious as he took a seat beside his wife, "you will apply to me, and I will sort him out."

"If there's sorting to be done, my lord, that office falls to me as His Grace's intended. I've encouraged him to resume writing his children's stories, for example."

Emmie was quietly exploding with joy, if her smile was any indication. Her ladyship had read the Christopher Dingle stories and been charmed by them. The tales worked well for children, and the prose was entertaining to adults as well. The wit was subtle and uproarious, and more than a bit irreverent.

Nicholas was eyeing the rest of the gingerbread loaf, which he could consume in its entirety as one of his fourteen afternoon snacks.

"Dunfallon has agreed to resume penning children's tales?" he asked.

"As my morning gift, I've requested a new kitten adventure, and I'm sure a second volume will be very well received. Christopher Dingle has a following, and we've been waiting years for more of his work."

"Have you met Dunfallon's sister?" Nicholas asked, edging his knee closer to the tea tray. "Impressive woman. Has three daughters, and in a very few years, they will be gracing the ballrooms."

Nick had just changed the subject, though he was among the most devoted of Christopher Dingle's followers. He'd read those stories to Leonie, the oldest daughter of the house, when she'd been in leading strings.

"Lady Crestwood will be at my open house," Lady Bellefonte said. "The one you will attend, along with your prospective spouse. I believe her ladyship is coming in part to watch her brother dodge all the mistletoe Nicholas is hanging in unavoidable locations."

"Please say you'll come." Nick took a sip of Lady Bellefonte's tea. "I want to see the look on Dunfallon's face when my brothers celebrate the season with you beneath that mistletoe."

"They won't find me lurking near the kissing boughs, my lord. I'll be assisting her ladyship to guard the gingerbread from hungry elves." Emmie rose. "I have tarried too long away from my duties, and I can see myself out. I'm busier than anticipated this holiday season, and there aren't enough hours in the day."

Lady Bellefonte stood and tugged her husband to his feet as well. "We'll both see you out, Emmie, and you—when next we are private —will regale me with an explanation for why a duke ended up sweeping the hearth at West Bart's Lending. I will hold the matter in confidence, but I am dying of curiosity."

"An interesting tale, I'm sure," his lordship said, all innocence.

"Shall I escort you back to the library, Miss Armstrong? Send a footman with you?"

"You shall not," Emmie replied. "I'm traveling exactly two genteel streets over, and one of the benefits of becoming socially obscure is that I can eschew some of Society's sillier rules. For now."

She was still beaming and blushing as she bustled out the door.

"So in love," Nick said. "Almost as in love as we are."

"You are enamored of the gingerbread on my tea tray and think to sweeten me up with flirtation. I neglected to serve myself a portion. For that reason only, you may accompany me back to the parlor."

"I am your most humble servant, though if you asked me to lug coal and sweep the hearths, I might be a bit... nonplussed."

"What was Dunfallon doing at a lending library, Nicholas? His castle probably has a library bigger than West and East Bart's combined."

Nick paused outside the parlor. "He was hiding, lovey. He dodged into West Bart's to avoid an encounter with Miss Peasegill. I waited half an hour for him to emerge, and yet, he tarried among the books. I understand why he'd enjoy a literary refuge, but I fear our Emerald is in for a rude shock."

Lady Bellefonte opened the parlor door. "He'd never play Emmie false, Nicholas. Duke or not, Dunfallon is a gentleman."

"He'd never play her false—not in that sense, especially not after this masquerading as a curate business—but he's also not about to resume writing children's stories. I've tried every way I know to get him to take up his pen again, but he's not having it. When a Scottish duke makes up his mind, only his granny or his conscience can make him change it, and Dunfallon has no living grannies."

Lady Bellefonte took her place on the sofa and gestured for her husband to close the parlor door. Nick complied, then came down beside her and curled an arm around her shoulders.

"Dunfallon dedicated his storybook to my Leonie," he said, referring her ladyship's step-daughter, who'd come into the world well before the marriage. "'To a very young lady of grace and charm.' He'd not met her, but she was his first critic, after me. You need a larger slice than that, lovey."

"This is your slice." She passed him his treat on a plate. "Why won't Dunfallon resume writing? His authorship has stayed secret for years, and it could surely remain so. Emmie seems to think more stories are both inevitable and to be prized above all other gifts. She's happy to marry the author, and willing to tolerate the ducal trappings that come with him."

"Emmie is bound for disappointment. Dunfallon says Spain changed him, but I think the loss of his brothers changed him more, and inheriting the title finished the job. He's entirely the lofty peer now, not a fanciful youth bent on literary rebellions. Why is your piece larger than mine?"

"Because, as God and all his herald angels know, I must keep up my strength."

"What about my strength?"

"Eat your gingerbread, Nicholas, and tell me why Spain or Waterloo or losing siblings would disincline Dunfallon to write more stories. He has the knack of crafting a tale that entertains and instructs without ever preaching."

Nick took a nibble of his gingerbread. He was a dainty eater, for all his size. "Dunfallon's father burned his stories, and that had to hurt like hell. To burn books your own son has written, lovely little stories about fluffy kittens and their intrepid feline adventures... I did not always understand my father, but I knew without doubt that he loved me in his way."

Lady Bellefonte poured herself another cup of tea. "My father hated me, and books were one of my few consolations. I hope His Grace does start writing again. That he resume the use of his talent would mean a great deal to Emmie."

Nicholas set aside his plate of half-eaten gingerbread. "I don't think it's that Dunfallon refuses to write more stories. I think it's that he *cannot*."

"That is a problem, given Emmie's expectations. Getting them to the altar will take more than mistletoe and kisses, Nicholas."

"I fear you are right, as usual, lovey mine. But speaking of kisses..."

"I saw you lock the door, sir. My holiday wish for Emmie and Dunfallon is that they are as prone to locking doors years after speaking their nuptial vows as we are."

"Don't neglect your gingerbread, lovey. You are soon to need *all* of your considerable strength."

Lady Bellefonte finished every crumb of her gingerbread.

CHAPTER SIX

"The house just wants some... warmth," Emmie said, frowning at a portrait of the fourth Duke of Dunfallon holding pride of place over the library mantel. "And a little less plaid, perhaps. You have plenty of books, and..."

Her voice trailed off as she studied the fourth duke, whom Dunfallon had always considered the merriest of a sober lot. The old fellow actually smiled. He held the reins of a muscular hunter with one hand. With the other, he stroked the head of an adoring brindle hound. The portrait had caught a happy moment in what surely must have been a happy life.

He'd been well-liked, a perennial favorite for Scotland's parliamentary delegation, and his nine children had had nothing but pleasant memories of him, if their diaries were to be believed.

"He has your nose," Emmie said, skimming glances between Dunfallon and his ancestor. "You have the same humor in your eyes. I suspect he read to his children, and his letters to his wife were tender and sweet."

"Papa burned those letters too. Claimed they were a lot of sentimental tripe unbecoming of a duke's dignity." Though they had been tender and sweet—also bawdy in places—and Secondus had copied the best of them before Papa could destroy them.

Dunfallon busied himself poking at the fire. In a room this size, even three hearths would need more than a day to chase off the chill, but Emmie had asked only yesterday to see the official Dunfallon town residence.

He would rather have had the staff tidying and dusting for a week, but the staff, such as it was, amounted to an elderly couple and their grumpy middle-aged son. All the dusting in the world would not get rid of too much plaid and too few comfortable places to sit.

"How many volumes do you have here?" Emmie said, slowly turning a circle.

"Too many that haven't been read in a century. I hope you are equal to the task of sorting the lot. I look in on the place from time to time, but it's not... I prefer more modest quarters."

"And the Albany doubtless likes the cachet of having you on the premises." Emmie took the poker from him, set it aside, and wrapped him in a hug. "When you are writing stories again, you will need two studies. One for when you are the duke and one for when you are the author."

She did this—dropped little references to his renewed efforts with a pen, and each one made Dunfallon feel more like a false suitor. She also bestowed lavish affection upon him—hugs, caresses, kisses to his cheek—and that made him joyous and a little wary.

He gave her a squeeze and stepped back. "Would you like to see the ducal suite?" They'd already toured the cellars, kitchen, pantries, and maids' quarters, along with endless parlors. Mr. and Mrs. Peyton were off visiting a cousin and they'd taken their grumpy son with them, so this reconnaissance mission was blessedly private.

"I'd like to see everything. The music room, the sewing room, the apartment you had in your youth. The whole lot."

"Then see it, you shall." He led her by the hand from the library, which was more of a book museum than a place to read and repose, and took down a lamp from a sconce. On a winter afternoon, the house was frigid and gloomy. Young Peyton—a mere lad of fifty-some —had lit a few candles, which made the corridor feel even darker.

"You don't have good memories of this place," Emmie said.

"London was a challenge. Papa brought us down from Scotland to show us off and to subject us to tea dances, though dancing for Secondus became unsupportable. We were to do the pretty, charm everybody, and uphold the family honor without exception."

"You were making a perpetual come out," Emmie said as they mounted the stairs. "My aunt uses that phrase to refer to the ladies who are dragged by the heels from the schoolroom at barely seventeen and still among the hopefuls five years later."

"Were you counted in that number?"

"My parents' deaths meant I was spared until the antediluvian age of nineteen, but the five years among the ferns and wallflowers applies. Then word got around that I had decent settlements—thank you, dear Auntie—and the bachelor midges began to swarm."

"Speaking of settlements, I should meet with your brother or send my solicitors to meet with his."

"I'd rather you met with Aunt."

They traversed another shadowed corridor and stopped before a carved oak door.

"I am calling upon your aunt tomorrow," Dunfallon said. "Will you be there?"

Emmie traced the horn of a rearing unicorn on the door panel. "I should be at West Bart's."

She moved her fingertips over the smooth curve of the creature's neck, the sweep of his back, the muscular curve of his rump, and Dunfallon was abruptly aware—very aware—that he was alone with his intended and about to step into the private suite of rooms where they would, heaven bless the notion, spend many a night together.

And possibly some afternoons, the occasional morning, and the odd predinner nap.

"Emmie, how much time do you spend at West Bart's Lending?"

She ceased caressing the rampant beast. "A fair bit."

He moved closer. "Emmie?"

"I'm there most days, at some point. I open and close most of the time. The library is not open on the Sabbath, of course, but the rest of the week, people need to read. Let's have a look at the ducal suite, shall we?" She lifted the latch and sailed ahead of him into a surprisingly warm space.

The fires were more effective here, or Mrs. Peyton's supervision of her menfolk more apparent. The hearth was blazing, and the screens had been moved to flank the windows, blocking the worst sources of drafts.

Emmie chafed her hands before the flames and scowled at the painting of Dunfallon Castle in all its craggy splendor above the mantel.

"Why so few pictures of family, Dane?"

"Papa allowed no pictures of family outside the gallery at Dunfallon Castle, but I had the fourth duke dusted off to keep an eye on the library. He's the forebearer I am most proud of. Wouldn't hear of clearances, while my own father..."

She held out a hand to him, and he took it. "Your father cleared his tenants from the land?"

"We own a pair of islands, and yes, he cleared the one. Engaged in the proverbial midwinter evictions, complete with sobbing women, howling babies, and shivering children. The steward was able to see that every family's possessions were transported to the mainland, and he settled any who wanted to remain in Scotland as best he could—a total of eleven families. The other six were given passage to Nova Scotia and as many coins as I could spare. At sixteen, I hadn't all that many coins."

The warmth of the room faded, replaced by memories of the bitter salt-sea air, and Papa sitting snug in his coach, watching a bedraggled parade of former tenants troop off the dock and into a bewildering and difficult future.

"All for his bloody sheep," Dunfallon added quietly.

Another memory joined the bleak assemblage in his mind. "The old women, one by one, spit upon Papa's fine coach. They were no longer his tenants and not on his land, so he could do nothing by way of retribution. Instead, he fired the steward that day, before those seventeen families, citing unreliable loyalty as the unpardonable sin."

"What did you do?"

"I stormed off to university and wrote stories about kittens. I came into a competence at seventeen and set up a decent pension for our former steward. His son is the current steward. When MacAlpin wasn't drilling me on my Roman philosophers, I tasked him with locating our departed tenants. Nine of the families who remained in Scotland have since returned to the island. Sheep, as it turned out, are a poor investment."

Emmie settled into a wing chair. "I thought Scotland and Wales were awash in sheep."

"In England and Wales, the climate allows for some variety in the breeds, but for my family's holdings, only the hardiest stock can stand up to the winters. Those sheep produce coarse, cheap wool, and because every laird and landowner is now raising sheep—the crofters having all been chased off the land they farmed profitably for centuries—the market is glutted. The military—now at peace—was the largest single purchaser of finer wool, so the higher-grade products are also glutted. Then too, any country can find a breed of sheep adapted to its climate, so wool exports have also declined."

Emmie made a lovely picture seated beside the fire. Dunfallon took the second chair without asking her permission. They were to be husband and wife, after all.

Also duke and duchess.

"Are those nine families happy?" she asked.

"They are struggling, but I am determined that they will eventually thrive. Sheep are a blight on the land, and in another few years, the damage would have been irreversible. We're making progress, but reclaiming the island is slow going."

Emmie unfastened the frogs of her cloak. "I wanted to see this house because we will live here at least part of the time. I thought I would come away from our tour with happy imaginings about re-stocking the library and donating older titles to West Bart's. I gather you'd like more than the library taken in hand."

She was clearly keen on managing the library, at least. That left only fourteen other rooms abovestairs immured in plaid.

"I was hoping," Dane said, "that you might, that is... new wall-paper in the music room, fresh curtains in the family parlor. The touches that can banish ghosts and turn a museum into a home."

Emmie wrinkled her nose. "This is important to you?"

"I hadn't put it that way, but yes. The house reeks of my father's grand consequence, and yet, I haven't the resolve or the time to tackle the changes needed."

"New appointments as well?" She still sounded less than enthusiastic.

"Carpets too, if you're up to that. I had thought to hire a deco-rator but I don't want my home to look decorated, I want it to look as West Bart's does—inviting, dignified, comfortable, secure." He fell silent rather than lapse into pleading.

"Very well," Emmie said, smiling slightly. "I will besiege the house, but don't be surprised if every room ends up with at least one shelf of good books."

"You may buy out every stall in Bloomsbury, and put bookshelves on every landing, and in the servants' hall. I was also hoping you might like to see the bedroom."

Now, where had *that* come from?

"A cheering thought, the bedroom. As you explain to me about sheep and evictions and burned love letters, I am gradually realizing that I will be a duchess. Sorting through the library here will be the least of the tasks expected of me, won't it?"

Dunfallon rose and offered Emmie his hand. "We will go on as we please, my dear. You can expect sweet, tender correspondence from me, I assure you. I regard Papa's greatest redeeming feature to be his use as a bad example. I may not have a clear idea of how I will execute the duties of my station, but I know how I will *not* go on."

Emmie kept a grip on his hand after she'd risen. "You will write more wonderful stories, for one thing."

That again. "I will not evict loyal tenants. I will not insist on being part of the parliamentary delegation to ensure that my interests take precedence over those of my equally deserving neighbors. I will not expect our children, should we be blessed with offspring, to puppet about Mayfair in tartan get-up while they spread lavish falsehoods about the wonders of the family coffers or our Scottish holdings."

He tugged her into his embrace, and she bundled close with wonderful enthusiasm. "This will be a happy household, Dunfallon. If it is within my power to make it so, we will have happy households. You will need peace and quiet for your writing, but if the children come along—and I pray they do—we will also have laughter, and raids on the gingerbread, and music, and love."

What courage she had, to envision so sanguine a future for them.

"And what of your own stories, hmm?" he asked, speaking with his lips against her temple. "Will you need two parlors, and will you write under a dashing pseudonym?"

Emmie eased away. "Let's have a look at the bedroom, shall we? I'm dying to see how the bed compares to the sofa in my office." She opened the door to the next room and disappeared from sight.

Dunfallon was left wondering what she could possibly mean—comparing the ducal bed and the office sofa—and hoping she meant what he thought she meant.

Being a duchess in theory was one thing. Every girl of means and standing was raised to envision herself with a circlet of jewels sparkling atop her head. The fairy-tale duchess wore gossamer clothing, spoke only in the sweetest tones, and uttered only wise, kind, or clever words.

She did not fall asleep among the biographies. She did not come to her exalted station at such an advanced age that half her child-bearing years were behind her. She did not spend most of every weekday at West Bart's Lending, the closest thing she'd had to a home in recent years.

These thoughts followed Emmie into the bedroom, as did a few hollow platitudes.

Every bride had misgivings.

Every *ducal* bride doubtless brought a duchy's worth of doubts with her to the altar and never mentioned one of them.

Long courtships were for couples who lacked the means to establish their own households.

And yet, when she beheld the ducal bed, a commotion ensued in her belly. She would spend her nights for a significant portion of her remaining years in this luxurious enormity.

"It's huge." As large as many a housekeeper's parlor, the bed curtains the blue and white of the Scottish saltire. The counterpane was more blue and white with touches of gold and rose. "One expects hot-air balloons to float about beneath the canopy."

Dunfallon had come into the room and closed the door. He used a taper to light two candelabra on the mantel and a third on the bedside table.

"I had this room made over in blue, white, and rose, which were my mother's favorite colors. The late duke was for waving plaid about on every occasion. I've nothing against plaid, but as a decorating theme, it becomes busy in small doses."

"Hence the library."

"And the servants' hall, the first formal parlor, the second formal parlor, the family parlor... I promised myself I would never wear a damned kilt once I became the duke."

Emmie moved a blue silk-covered pillow near the head of the bed so the arrangement was symmetric. "Now that is a shame. I'm as susceptible to the charm of a kilted laddie as the next woman."

Dunfallon tossed the taper onto the crackling fire in the hearth. "You are as impressionable as Aberdeen granite, Emerald

Armstrong." He prowled closer. "For you, I'd put on the whole kit, provided you assisted me to get out of it."

Touring the house had been a bad idea. With each room visited, Emmie had felt her spirit sinking and her confidence as well.

The porcelain *room*—not a porcelain cabinet.

The silver *room*—not a silver chest.

The *third* formal parlor, reserved for receiving bankers, solicitors, and stewards representing other peers.

But the bedroom reminded her of a singular and comforting fact: She was marrying Tertius Dane MacManus MacTavish Dundee—she'd made a little tune to help her recall all those names—and he was a very dear and desirable man.

Emmie leaned near enough to whisper. "I will assist you to remove the ensemble you're wearing right this moment, if you're amenable, Your Grace."

"Dane," he said, drawing her into a hug. "When private, or anytime you please, my name is Dane. Are you intent on ravishing me, Miss Armstrong?"

"Is that hope I hear in your voice?"

"Is that worry in yours? I did not bring you here to enable a seduction, Emmie. We'll have to make a home of this place, and I rely on you to guide that process."

"We will also have to make a marriage in this place, among others, and engaged couples are expected to anticipate their vows." Emmie hadn't planned to tryst with Dane on this inspection tour, but how much more important was it that they inspect *each other* rather than a lot of parlors and pantries?

He sat on the enormous cloud-bed, where he looked entirely at ease. "Join me, and we will talk about this marriage of ours."

Emmie was seized by a desperate reluctance to talk. She would analyze her motives for propositioning her intended later, probably a dash of bridal nerves, braided with a pragmatic need to get the first encounter behind them, and a touch of fear that, unless she took this step now, her courage might falter.

And if she dithered, then Dane might decide that a bluestocking duchess wasn't such a fine idea after all.

As Emmie settled beside him on the bed, her feet a good ten inches from the floor, she admitted that her duke was... formidable. Lord Hercules had not been formidable. He'd been arrogant and underhanded, and Emmie hadn't understood the difference.

Dane was not arrogant. He was kind and patient, and lovely, and —did this even signify to him?—a successfully published author.

"Does one negotiate the ravishment of one's prospective husband?" Emmie asked, hands folded in her lap.

"One discusses a significant step to be taken with one's prospective wife, because it's not a step that can be untaken, Emmie. How awful was the fumbling Lord Hercules?"

"I haven't any way to assess that. I did not enjoy his attentions, and Aunt says that means he mucked it up beyond all recall. I do enjoy your attentions—so far."

Dunfallon looped an arm around her shoulders. "Promise me something."

"I'm listening."

"Promise me that if you are uncomfortable for any reason—the light is in your eyes, you don't like where my hands are, you don't care for the position, I'm going too slowly or too quickly—don't let matters get to the beyond-all-recall stage before you demand an intermission, Emmie."

She was bundled against his side, a wonderful place to be, and yet, she had questions too. "How long do you expect this to take?"

He brushed a kiss to her temple. "Until early spring, if I had my way, but alas, half the afternoon will have to do."

The commotion in Emmie's belly became a full-blown riot. "Half the afternoon?"

"At least."

"I suppose we'd best get started."

Dane laughed and rose from the bed.

Dunfallon had spoken the truth. His intention had been to show Emmie the house, nothing more. That she had taken it into her head to consummate their courtship left him...

Pleased, of course. He cared for her deeply and desired her madly, and she was right: Even in polite society, couples typically engaged in intimacies on the way to the altar. Emmie knew that all too well.

And yet, something about the quality of her determination made him uneasy. She did not appear overcome with lust for his person, and she had not planned this assignation—he would bet his Shakespeare First Folio on that.

Some notion had taken hold of her, a now-or-never sort of desperation, and Dunfallon honestly could not decide where the honorable course lay.

If he rejected her overtures, she'd be hurt. The strutting-male part of him also loudly bellowed that he'd be a fool to deny himself shared pleasure with his intended when she was sitting on the very bed.

If he consummated their courtship, and Emmie did not care for the experience, where would that leave her? The answer hit him like the flat of a claymore to the chest: She'd be free to *change her mind*. To go back to her books and prodigies and leave Dane to the dubious joys of duking.

"Let's start with your hooks, shall we?"

Emmie's gaze turned wary. "My hooks?"

"If we are to all the pleasures prove in that bed, then shedding our clothes comes into it. The room is toasty, I'll warm the sheets, and then we will set the mattress aflame."

Emmie rose and gave him her back. "I wasn't sure. Hercules favored perching me on tables or bending me over the nearest chair."

Lord Hercules was about to lose his coach and four and his favorite riding horse over a polite hand of cards. Polite, but not friendly. If Hercules was foolish enough to accept an invitation to spar at Jackson's, his losses might include a few teeth as well.

"The bed for us," Dunfallon said, stroking his thumbs over Emmie's bare nape. "Lots of pillows, a pleasant nap between romps, soothing caresses, and passionate kisses." He pressed a lingering example of same to her nape. "All the time in the world."

"You'll use your toothpowder?"

Ye mischievous fairies, Lord Hercules deserved to lose a testicle. "Of course, and you are welcome to borrow my toothbrush as well. This suite is kept in readiness for me no matter how reluctant I've been to dwell here."

Emmie's dress was simple, the buttons fewer than Dunfallon would have found on a more fashionable creation. He loosened her corset strings while he was making himself useful and treated himself to lazy kisses along her shoulder.

"You're sure, Emmie?"

"Oh, yes. Very sure." She sounded determined rather than enthusiastic.

"Why don't you nip behind the privacy screen, and I'll get out of my boots?"

She turned, hugged him, and rustled off to the corner screened by a japanned panel. Again, her air was not that of a woman anticipating a pleasurable interlude, but rather, that of a nervous bride.

Perhaps, Dunfallon thought as he divested himself of all but his breeches, Lord Hercules should lose the deed to his house too. But no, probably not. Lady Hercules was already serving penance enough.

Dunfallon ran the warmer over the sheets, heard water splashing against porcelain, and reveled in a sense of humming desire. Good fortune had given him a bride intent on sorting matters out before she found herself married to a bumbler, and this was simply more proof that Emmie would be a spectacular duchess as well as a wonderful wife.

She deserved to try his paces, and she deserved—more than

deserved—to change her mind if she found him wanting.

Which, centuries of bred-in-the-bone Highland pride thundered, *he would not be.*

"Your turn." Emmie had emerged from the privacy screen wearing her chemise and a banyan of green silk that did marvelous things for her eyes. Her hair was a dark braid over one shoulder, and her feet were bare. She studiously avoided any glances at the vast bed or at Dunfallon's naked chest.

Tenderness cut through his desire, or rather, blended with it. "That dressing gown looks much better on you than it ever did on me. Give me two minutes."

He spent closer to five, making liberal use of the toothpowder, washing *everywhere* for good measure, and dragging a brush through his hair.

When he emerged from the privacy screen, Emmie was standing by the bed, looking pensive and precious.

He loved her. Loved her courage and pragmatism. Loved her disdain for polite society's games. Loved her affectionate nature and her devotion to her causes. He held out his arms, and she bundled into his embrace.

"I'm nervous, Dane. I'm trying to pretend to a sophistication I cannot claim. You are right that Hercules was... distasteful. He was brusque and hurried and less than particular about his hygiene."

Dunfallon was coming to love the way they fit together and to treasure the bodily trust Emmie showed him. He positively hated Lord Hercules.

"I'd cheerfully kill him for you, my dearest, but murder charges would interfere with our honey month. I suppose ruining him will have to do."

"You can do that?" She sounded hopeful, bless her.

"In the space of seventy-two hours, I will wreck him, foot, horse, and cannon, if you like."

She sighed, and Dunfallon felt some of the anxiety flow out of her. "Lord Hercules's ruin is a cheering thought—I consoled myself with dreams of his downfall for months—then I began to write fiction instead. Dashing cads never end well in my tales. I'd rather you spend your energies writing more kitten stories, Dane."

He stroked her back and wondered how much literature had been born of an author's sense of discontent and defeat.

"Dashing cads should never prevail," he said, "and dashing damsels should always win the day—and the duke." He kissed her, hoping discussions of Lord Hercules and blasted kittens could be set aside once and for all.

And thank the celestial powers, Emmie kissed him back. Dunfallon was developing a sorting system for her kisses. The peck on the cheek signaled he'd said something she approved of. The gentler buss indicated he'd tugged at her heartstrings. The smacker conveyed lustier joy...

Emmie wielded words well, but she was an orator with kisses.

In the ducal bedroom, she added blatant passion to her repertoire, taking a taste of him and then daring him to reciprocate. Though desire rode Dunfallon hard, he tried to go slowly and considerately, to be all that Ham-fisted Hercules had not been.

"I'm panting," Emmie said, linking her hands at Dunfallon's nape. "I'm panting like the heroines in all the Gothic novels. I do believe my bosom is actually heaving."

She studied the indicated part of her anatomy, as did Dunfallon —for about two mesmerizing seconds.

"You are so wonderful," he said, scooping her into his arms. "I want the whole of you heaving and panting and sighing. I want you shouting your pleasure to the rafters and then demanding the same again only better." He settled her on the bed, peeled out of his breeches, and came down over her.

"I want that too," she said, "providing you are heaving and panting as well."

He kissed her nose. "I am already panting. Kiss me some more, Emmie."

She kissed, she caressed, she sniffed, and stroked, and explored, and Dunfallon's grasp of reason began to unravel.

"This is why you said we'll be here half the afternoon, isn't it?" Emmie asked, straddling him. "Because there's so much more than hurried couplings behind the parlor door."

"Hurried couplings behind the parlor door can be delightful," Dunfallon said, tracing her breasts through the soft linen of her chemise. "An unexpected bit of heaven. With you, I want everything. The stolen moments, the sleepy joys, the towering passion. I want quiet nights by the fire and rousing political arguments over break-fast. I want... I want *you*, Emmie. All of you, and I want to give you all of me."

He wanted her in the next five minutes and for the next fifty years—at least. She curled down to his chest and snuggled close.

"The things you say, Dane. Now my heart is heaving."

So was his, and among the wishes and thoughts bobbing around on his emotional sea was a regret. Nobody had ever loved Papa like this, clearly, or the old fool would not have gone so far astray from what really mattered. For all his wealth and consequence, the previous duke had died unmourned and alone, and worse, he had probably died lonely without even realizing it.

"I love you," Dunfallon said, gathering Emmie closer. "I love you madly, Emerald Armstrong."

"And I love you, Dane MacTavish Dundee and all those other names that have flown straight out of my head. Someday I will slip and call you Mr. Dingle in a muddled moment."

"Just please not Tertius," he said, though her mention of Mr. Dingle sent a wisp of misgiving through him. "Emmie, I think you should know I'm unlikely to ever again write children's stories."

"Nonsense." She kissed his chest. "We'll make time for that, Dane. I realize that you're a very busy man, peer of the realm, manhood's finest flower, et cetera and so forth. But you've put off taking up your pen for too long. A hundred other peers can make speeches in Parliament. Only you can write more kitten stories."

"No, I cannot." He needed for her to understand this. "Like you,

I wrote out of discontent with matters beyond my control. That is behind me now, and rather than writing silly little stories, I have other means of exerting my influence."

Emmie angled up, using her elbow on his chest for leverage. "Silly... little... stories? Are you quoting your father?"

"Not intentionally. Just because he was a martinet doesn't mean he was always wrong." And in that pronouncement, Dunfallon had indeed sounded ominously like dratted Papa.

Emmie dismounted and sat beside Dunfallon, the covers swaddling her to her armpits. "But you are a *writer*. A brilliant, gifted, clever, published writer. You cannot walk away from that."

Dunfallon sat up as well rather than lounge around on his back when Emmie was apparently off on some female flight of illogic.

"I already have walked away." That statement had come across as disdainful, so Dunfallon tried to explain. "I was *marched* away from my literary ambitions years ago, Emmie. Lectured at length on the folly of those aspirations while my personal copies of the book were burned before my eyes. My associations with published authordom are not cheering, and I do not intend to renew my literary efforts."

"How can you sound like a duke even when you aren't wearing a stitch?" she muttered, worrying a nail.

How could she carp on Dunfallon's youthful folly when she was all but naked in their bed?

"Emmie, I *am* a duke. As you've said, some things cannot be helped. I have the ear of the Regent, I dine on occasion with Wellington, I have connections in many a foreign court, thanks to my tour of duty in Vienna. These privileges make it incumbent upon me to spend my time on affairs that matter—bills, parliamentary committees, estate problems. Intrepid kittens are no longer on my schedule."

Tell me you understand.

Tell me you are disappointed but bow to my unassailable reasoning.

Tell me you love me.

Emmie flipped back the covers and hopped off the bed.

CHAPTER SEVEN

Tell him you understand, Emmie's conscience bellowed. *Tell him he's not wrong, though you are disappointed to agree with his conclusions. Tell him again that you love him.*

"I must think about this," she said, making straight for the privacy screen. "I must... I simply assumed that you would write more of those wonderful stories. But then, I assumed Lord Hercules cared for me. I assumed my settlements were a secondary consideration for him. I assumed—however briefly—that you were a particularly fashionable curate, and I further assumed I could adjust to becoming a duchess."

Dunfallon folded his arms over the top of the privacy screen, all lazy masculine grace and bare, broad shoulders.

"Emmie, please don't turn a minor misunderstanding into some great drama. You appreciate my stories, and I'm glad you do, but there's more to me now than little feline fables. Of necessity, there must be."

Emmie regarded her reflection, a rosy, rumpled version of herself who had been having a *delightful* time in the sky-blue bed with her intended.

Meet him halfway, you henwit. Don't storm off in high dudgeon.

"You are attempting patient reason with me, Dunfallon." She was attempting patient reason with herself, too, and failing to achieve the desired result.

"Forgive me if I appeal to logic, Emmie, but I grasp how much I ask of you when I invite you to be my wife. Even if we refuse most invitations, we will still be subjected to interminable court functions, formal dinners, endless processions of guests during shooting season, most of whom we cannot in any capacity regard as friends. Gossip about infidelities neither of us has committed, fawning from syco-phants who can't even bother to be witty."

This recitation turned his expression bleak and suggested to Emmie that, in some ways, Dunfallon was still the lonely, bewildered youth who'd been sent off to learn the manly art of patriotic slaughter in Spain.

"Doubts on your part are only to be expected," he said, straight-ening, "but please don't drag my adolescent literary rebellion into the affray. To be very honest, it's not that I refuse to write more stories, it's that I cannot."

"Of course you can."

He wandered away, probably to put on a shirt and breeches, and that... that disappointed Emmie. They were having a proper row—one she'd started—and clothing was a sort of armor worn in the marital lists. She used some chilly wash water, then wiggled her corset on over her chemise and brought the strings to the front for the usual maiden-lady compromise between fashion and pragmatism.

"Let me do that," Dunfallon said, prowling around the screen, fully attired save for his coat. "When you are my duchess, I will perform this courtesy frequently, and while we are airing opinions, you need to know that I am an enthusiastic appreciator of the natural female shape."

He laced her up with just the right touch of snugness and then held her dress over her head. Because of his superior height, he could work the garment down in tidy stages. Emmie was soon fully clothed, though her hair needed attention.

"Please have a seat at the vanity," he said. "I can manage a chignon, and not because I've enjoyed a string of exotic mistresses. My older sister liked for me to brush out her hair when I was quite small."

Emmie perched on the vanity stool. "As a bachelor duke, exotic mistresses were your due."

"Do I take from your tone that a married duke isn't to indulge in such frolics?"

"You absolutely do."

"Good," he replied, undoing her braid, "because I have no intention of being a fashionable husband in that regard. I proposed to you because I esteem you, Emmie. I esteem your integrity and your character. I'm sorry the afternoon hasn't gone as planned. I'm glad we can be honest with each other."

He *esteemed* her. Not long ago, he'd said he loved her, and the difference in the words wasn't half so troubling as the difference in the tone with which he'd spoken them.

"In the spirit of honesty, Your Grace, you need to know that I am disappointed in your decision to stop writing for the children." To turn his back on the part of him that had first captured Emmie's heart, and that she'd been so sure would make them close companions as well as a devoted couple.

He wielded the brush with competence and care. No lingering caresses, no little pauses for kisses or whispered endearments.

And that is my fault.

"In the course of a long and loving marriage, my dearest, I'm sure we will weather occasional disappointments, but we will remain allies and friends." He separated her hair into three skeins and began a braid that curled over her right shoulder.

"Your parents were not friends or allies?"

Dunfallon paused in his plaiting. "I hardly recall. Mama had presented Papa with an heir and two spares, though she'd had the bad form to start off with my older sister. The duchess had earned a certain measure of independence. When I was eight, she died of a lung fever, and I have few memories of her before that. Her death did not change life at the castle all that much."

He resumed braiding, and Emmie was assailed by the urge to cry. Nobody had read stories to the youngest Dunfallon son, that was certain.

"You think your kitten tales don't matter," Emmie said, "but they do."

"They are pleasant little bagatelles useful for sending children docilely to sleep when a tired parent reaches the end of the day." He plucked the hair ribbon off the vanity and tied a secure knot. "I do not flatter myself that I accomplished more than that. Are we still engaged, Emmie?"

He began fashioning a bun at her nape, as briskly as if he were her usual coiffeur and she preparing for yet another evening entertainment.

"Why wouldn't we be?"

"Because you are disappointed in me."

While Dunfallon silently pinned her hair into a bun, Emmie considered that proposition. "It's worse than that. I am bewildered by you." And to some extent by herself, because he was right. She was making drama out of proportion to the moment, but she was also genuinely stunned that he'd belittle his own creations.

He finished and stood behind her with his hands on her shoulders. "Can you explain your bewilderment?"

To pose a question rather than make a demand had doubtless cost him some pride. Emmie realized her pride was also involved, if not the driving force behind this whole altercation.

Pride had a place in marriage, but arrogance did not, and she owed Dunfallon honesty—his word.

"Books saved my life, Your Grace. I had no desire at all to be launched into Society, but Aunt insisted that marrying was my first responsibility when my brother and I emerged from mourning. She explained that if I was mooning about the ancestral pile, the most desirable parties would pass over Ambrose because his sister already held the reins at the family seat. Getting leg-shackled was to be my salvation and my duty."

Dunfallon took a seat on the chest at the foot of the bed, and Emmie turned on the stool to face him.

"And you failed at that duty for five years?" he said.

"Failed miserably. I was the butt of jokes, the subject of wagers. I was the despair of my aunt and handed around from one modiste and milliner to another. All of them attempted outlandish experiments in an effort to cast me as an original. They turned me into a freak. One of them insisted that I be laced so tightly I fainted at Lady Dandridge's Venetian breakfast, and the talk only grew worse from there."

"I'm sorry."

"I do not want your pity. I want your understanding—your comprehension."

Something cool and wary came into his gaze. "Go on."

"In all these years," Emmie said, "the years of mourning, the years of social tribulation, the years since my only other suitor tossed me over, I've had the consolation and inspiration of books. Not only fiction, Dunfallon. I've read Mary Wollstonecraft, despite the scurrilous drivel her late husband heaped on her memory. I've read Sir William Blackstone's commentaries on many aspects of the law. I've read poetry and travelogues and fables and novels."

"You are a bluestocking. I like this about you. I enjoy good literature too."

Despair joined the bewilderment wrapped around Emmie's heart. "I owe *my life* to books, Dunfallon, and I mean those words in their least flattering sense. When Lord Hercules threw me over and then put it about that the fault had been mine, I ran out of fortitude. I stopped eating. I stopped going out. I would not receive the visitors who came to tour the ruins of my life. I lay in bed by the day and the week, and I longed to die."

"You? And your brother *allowed* this?"

"I lived with my aunt, and Ambrose and I had grown apart. There was no *allowing*, Dunfallon. Even a duke cannot force a woman to eat, to care about a life that proved over and over that she was a failure at everything."

He looked genuinely puzzled, and as if he was perhaps resisting the urge to argue. "You were in a bad way."

"And you are being kind. I was a wreck, but Aunt insisted I leave my rooms at least often enough for the maids to clean. I sought refuge in her library, and Aunt is well-read. That's where I found Wollstonecraft, who paints a very different picture of polite society's treatment of women than I'd been raised to understand. I found Mrs. Burney, who in her fashion said the same things Mrs. Wollstonecraft had said. I found that rascal Lord Rochester, and despite all, his vulgar, clever poetry made me laugh. I found Mr. Dingle's stories and his unrelenting faith that there is always a way home, if only we are resourceful and true to ourselves and to our loved ones."

Emmie stopped speaking rather than descend into ranting. The bleak eternity after her broken engagement had piled in on top of mourning, loneliness, homesickness, and that terrible row with Ambrose, and the only beacon of joy in the whole gloomy heap had been books.

And most of those, according to Dunfallon, had been *silly little stories*. He did not understand, and *of all people*, he should.

"Don't cry, Emmie, please don't..." Dunfallon passed her a handkerchief redolent of that majestic-forest scent Emmie associated with him. "Please don't... Your tears break my heart."

"Those *little feline fables*," she said in a low, determined voice, "gave me a way home when I had no home, when all of me, not only my heart, was broken. You belittle and malign those stories at your peril, Dunfallon—you break *my* heart—and you turn your back on the ability to write more of them when I know how very, very important such stories are."

He rose and drew her to her feet and then into his arms. "You are important to me," he said. "I am so sorry that life brought you that low."

Emmie allowed herself to rest against him, because this recitation, this argument, had conjured too vivid a recollection of that old seductive darkness and despair. Safety and sanity had been rebuilt one book at a time, one outing to the quiet order of the library at a time.

Then had come the magical day when Emmie had attempted to write a story of her own.

"Life brings many of us low, Dunfallon. Illness, misfortune, broken hearts, a ducal ass for a father, and we can bear it if we're not alone and if we can find a way home. I did, you did. That matters."

He'd asked her a question: Were they still engaged? Emmie wanted to say yes, to say that this painful discussion had brought them closer, and they were more engaged than ever. But if intrepid kittens were no longer on his schedule, that left only the busy duke to become her husband.

The busy duke, along with carpets, wallpaper, appointments, curtains, and—heaven help her—formal occasions of state.

Emmie remained silent in Dunfallon's embrace, weary to her soul. The man who'd read stories to small children, who had *written* those stories, and who had patiently hung greenery over the library door, had been a passing ghost. A figment of Emmie's imagination and Dunfallon's holiday sentiments. The duke himself did not love books—he *enjoyed good literature.*

She feared very much that she and His Grace, as lovely and dear as he was, would not suit.

~

"So how did you leave it wi' yer lassie?" MacAlpin asked, passing Dunfallon a wee dram.

"Awkwardly. I kissed her cheek, and she suffered my attention before bidding me good day." The memory stung, but not nearly as hard as the memory of Emmie recounting her worst, lowest moments. Years of grief, Society's cruelty, and loneliness had reduced a lioness to lurking in her lair with only her miseries—and some books—for company.

"What the hell is wrong with her brother, MacAlpin? Where was his handsome young lordship when his sister needed a strong arm to lean upon?"

MacAlpin lowered his considerable bulk into the opposite wing chair. This study had been crated up, down to the last quill pen and ink pot, and carted from Perthshire to Oxford and then to London. The chairs were familiar, as was the portrait of the mighty stag on his misty Highland crag.

So, too, was the sense that Dunfallon had come to this place to sort out a life that baffled him, though his last visit to MacAlpin's study had been prior to his departure for Spain. In recent years, he and MacAlpin met for dinner at MacAlpin's literary club or strolled amiably in the park on sunny mornings. They even took tea in Mrs. Mac's parlor.

At some point, they had stopped conferring over Dunfallon whiskies in MacAlpin's masculine sanctuary.

"And just how useful were you to your sister?" MacAlpin asked. "Her ladyship had a hard road, and she also lost her mama too soon."

"*Slàinte.*" Dunfallon took a diplomatic sip of very smooth whisky. Her ladyship was eight years his senior, a law unto herself, and had been determined to quit the castle on the arm of the first remotely eligible suitor.

Which she had done, much to her youngest brother's heartbroken dismay.

"I was a boy," Dunfallon muttered. "Lord Threadham is a peer of the realm."

"Whose sister you intend to marry, without bothering to discuss the matter with him."

MacAlpin had many fine qualities, from a hearty singing voice to a fine sense of humor. He was patience personified around fidgety boys, and he could quote Shakespeare by the scene. At some point during Dunfallon's university education, MacAlpin, accompanying him as his personal tutor, had also acquired the credentials of a prosy old bore.

Since that time, his hair had turned snow-white, his beard had become luxuriant, and his eyes—if anything—more blue.

"You have attained curmudgeonhood, MacAlpin."

"Oh, aye. Mrs. MacAlpin beat me past the post in that regard, but she does set me a fine example. What will you do about your duchess, lad?"

"She's not my duchess yet." And some traitorous, logical part of Dunfallon wondered if that was for the best. A peer of the realm, a duke, fifty-ninth in line for the throne—or maybe sixty-eighth or seventy-third—did not sit about on his backside spinning fanciful tales for children. "I know she's begun to harbor doubts of the you-do-me-great-honor variety."

"Miss Armstrong was cast aside once before, you know." MacAlpin lifted his glass. "*Slàinte mhath.*"

"The gossips put the boot on the other foot," Dunfallon said, "though you have the right of it. Lord Hercules treated her cruelly, and dealt a final blow to her spirits after years of buffeting. He treats a woman—a tender-hearted, valiant woman, a lady worth more than rubies—as if she were the party found wanting."

"You're listening to gossips now, laddie?"

"They will insist on gossiping where I can hear them. I paid this call so I might listen to you. As much as I esteem my intended, I cannot allow Emmie to begin our marriage ordering me about."

MacAlpin nosed his glass and peered at the exposed ceiling beams. "Of course not, Lord Tertius."

"I haven't been Lord Tertius for ages."

Which was, of course, the point. Lord Tertius had had a ducal martinet for a father, few friends beyond his horse and MacAlpin's cats, and little ability to change his circumstances.

"I don't intend to order Emmie about either, if that makes a difference."

"Prudent of you. Mrs. Mac is always vastly entertained when I get to putting on airs. My strutting and snorting has her in a fine humor for days, though I can't say sleeping on yonder couch does much for my lumbago."

Usually, when MacAlpin was at his most vexatious, he was also at his most wise. Dunfallon had taken years to figure that out.

MacAlpin was being very vexatious.

"The stories I wrote can be excused as a youthful flight, the passing fancy of one not yet in line to inherit."

"You were always in line to inherit. Kevin was reckless and Secondus sickly. The old duke couldn't control his heir and couldn't cure his spare, so he whaled away on you all the harder. His version of preparing you for the title, I suppose. Fatherly devotion, however misguided. He would not listen to me, of course. No reasoning with a desperate duke."

Oh, that was subtle. "*Dùin do bheul*, MacAlpin."

"I'll no' be shuttin' my mouth until I've had my say, Your Dunder-headedness."

"I am all ears, hoping to nourish my flagging spirits with the ambrosia of your wisdom, also with some decent whisky."

"Then finish your whisky and heed me. Your stories are fine little tales."

Dunfallon waved a hand, though from MacAlpin that was high praise.

"They are also damned clever, because they said all the things your father could not hear. You were ready to enlist—to bloody enlist with the common soldiers, to take ship, to steal away with the traveling people—anything to escape your father's control. You know what it is to be much buffeted, laddie. You wrote your stories for all the folk out there feeling much buffeted, and you wrote them because you hurt like hell."

"I hurt worse in Spain." Too late, Dunfallon realized that he had not argued MacAlpin's assertion that the stories were more than passing amusements from a rebellious youth.

"No, you did not. The suffering in Spain was universal. The bitter cold, the violence, the blistering heat. Mr. Dingle's suffering was personal. Different business altogether." MacAlpin rose by slow heaves to fetch the decanter. "Goddamned winter is hell on an old man's bones."

Dunfallon had ever enjoyed his tutor's colorful language, though he'd also taken for granted that MacAlpin would always be *there*, always have a welcome for him, and a kind, if gruff, word. Watching the old man navigate around his sanctum brought a stab of sadness.

MacAlpin would not live forever, and then how would Lord Tertius, His Grace of Dunfallon, or Mr. Damned Dingle find his way home?

"You think I should resume writing, but, Mac, what would I write? I haven't had a decent story idea for years. Nothing I could come up with now would be any good."

"True. Everybody would laugh at you, assuming they learned of your pathetic little hobby."

Papa had called Dunfallon's writing a pathetic little hobby. "I could kick you."

"I can be fast when I have to be, and you, apparently, can still be quite slow. More whisky?"

"No, thank you, though I appreciate the hospitality. If I do marry Emmie, will you stand up with me?"

"Mrs. MacAlpin would be horrified if I were to so far forget my humble station. Get that giant earl fella to stand up with you. He's a decent sort."

"He will dwarf me at the altar, while you, in your Highland finery, will make a very fine picture."

"We'll see what Missus thinks on the matter, but from what you've said, the nuptials are in doubt. I rather admire a young lady who can see past the duke to the man, and to the boy the man used to be. Shows discernment. Too many young people today lack discernment."

"Please, MacAlpin, not the young-people-today tirade."

Dunfallon's host waggled the decanter in an admonitory fashion. "Be off with ye, lad. Stop by the stable to look in on wee Caspar before ye go. He's my favorite kind of boy—bright, stubborn, and determined. Missus adores him, and she has discernment by the barge-load. Witness, she married me."

Emmie adored Caspar, too, but did Emmie adore her intended? Dunfallon hoped she did, because he still very much adored her, which just made the whole situation hopelessly complicated.

"I'm for the stable, and you will give my love to Mrs. MacAlpin, please."

"Take on that fraught task yourself, my boy. She's in her parlor, knitting socks or spinning the fate of dukes. If you're thinking of scurrying off to the castle after the young lady dumps you, at least look in on us before your blow retreat."

"Dumps me?"

"Like a load of wrinkled ducal linen." MacAlpin raised his glass, winked, and downed the whole.

I am being dismissed. The experience had become novel, but Dunfallon bowed and took his leave like the good boy he'd once been. He made his obeisance before Mrs. MacAlpin, who insisted on sending him on his way with a packet of shortbread.

The day was bitterly cold and gray, though Dunfallon was in no hurry to return to the correspondence, ledgers, reports, and bills awaiting him in his bachelor quarters. The ever-so-important matters on which he squandered the bulk of his days.

Looking in on the boy would be a far better use of his time, and to blazes with the account books.

~

Dunfallon let himself through MacAlpin's back gate, crossed the alley, and entered the little stable that housed Mrs. MacAlpin's cart pony and Mac's old riding horse. They shared a roomy stall, the pony clearly the head of the household.

A few hens roosted in the rafters. A pair of nanny goats curled on a pile of straw in the second stall and chewed their cuds contently. The air was scented with hay, livestock, and leather, and while far from cozy, the stable had a snug feel.

Something about a stable in winter would always appeal to Dunfallon. He'd sought refuge in his father's stables, and at school, he'd often...

A twitch of movement caught his eye. Something white and furry slipped out from between the pony's hooves and leaped through the bars of the hayrack. A feline wound itself around Dunfallon's boots, purring madly.

"You're a friendly old thing."

She peered up at him out of jade-green eyes and slowly blinked. Not a young cat, a bit plump and saggy. A dowager queen. Dunfallon knelt to offer the requisite scratch about the ears, and the cat launched herself at his chest.

A shivery feeling passed over him as she grazed her cheek against his chin. "Jewel?" How many green-eyed white cats could MacAlpin own? "Are you my old Jewel?"

She licked his chin and tried to nuzzle her way inside his great-coat. The shivery feeling turned to joy out of all proportion to the moment. Jewel had been a snuggler as a kitten and as a young lady. She'd outgrown such undignified behavior when the tomcats had caught her eye.

"She's allowed the freedom of the city in winter," a young voice said. "The rest of the year, she's a house cat. MacAlpin says she's had enough kits to last her a lifetime. Her name's Jewel, like in the stories."

Caspar came down the ladder as nimbly as a squirrel. He was

108

cleaner than Dunfallon had ever seen him, and he'd lost the worst of
the gauntness in his cheeks.

"I like it out here," he went on. "The beasts are good company,
and Mrs. MacAlpin says Mister Mac is getting on and shouldn't try
to look after the chores all by hisself."

Caspar's speech had changed, acquiring a faint burr and much
more careful diction. MacAlpin was nothing if not a miracle worker.
But then, Mrs. Mac's shortbread also had wondrous qualities where
small boys were concerned.

"We miss you at the library," Dunfallon said, taking a seat on a
bench while the cat persisted in her efforts to investigate his
greatcoat.

"I miss West Bart's too," Caspar replied. "Missus says we can visit
on Thursday, though Mister Mac has nearly as many books as West
Bart's does. Did Miss Emmie send you?"

"Yes, in a sense."

"That cat sure does like you."

"And I like her. She was a friend when friends were few, and
she's apparently not forgotten her old chum."

"Our mates matter," Caspar said, brushing his fingers along the
cat's tail. "Mr. Dingle says that."

Dunfallon undid the top buttons of his coat, and Jewel secreted
herself next to his chest. Her proportions had changed, her purr
had not.

"Mac says I'm old enough to read anything I please for myself."
Caspar took the place beside Dunfallon on the bench, scuffing his
boots—new boots, from the look of them—on the dirt floor. "Mrs.
Mac says reading to me helps keep her eyes sharp. They are nice
people, but..."

"But you don't trust them," Dunfallon said. "I was about your age
when I met MacAlpin. He was big, loud, and used words I'd never
heard before, as if he was some kind of linguistic fencing master. I
knew not if he was a demon or an angel, so I decided I would watch

him closely and make up my mind when I had a better sense of his motives."

The recollection of those early days under MacAlpin's tutelage was both sweet and sad. Such a lonely boy, though any other child in the realm would probably have envied him.

"I should go," Dunfallon said to nobody in particular.

"Mr. Dingle says we oughtn't to try to solve a problem until we know all we can learn about it. Like when the bridge froze. The kittens didn't know if the river would ice up overnight, and they didn't know if cat snatchers lurked beneath the bridge... I woulda punched any cat snatchers where it counts, I can tell you that."

Cat snatchers figured prominently in Dingle's tales. Nasty, speechifying old men who stank of pipe smoke and frequently threatened to teach small kittens respect for their betters. The cat snatchers were invariably foiled, only to turn up more determined and odoriferous in the next story.

Jewel situated herself so she could peek out beneath Dunfallon's chin.

"If you give MacAlpin a chance to earn your trust, Caspar, you will not regret it. I consider him a friend."

Caspar glanced over at the goats, the skepticism of the ancients in his young eyes. "You ain't just sayin' that?"

"MacAlpin all but saved my life. He certainly saved my soul. Do you suppose wee Ralph might join you here, or Mary?"

"Mates stick together," Caspar said. "Mr. Dingle—"

Dunfallon rose. "Mr. Dingle is not the universal authority on all questions of substance, Caspar."

Caspar scowled. "He's a pretty smart feller, you ask me. O'Keefe the Thief tried to recruit me and Ralphie for his gang. We said no, because O'Keefe *ain't* loyal to his mates. He's rich, he has the watchmen in his pocket, and he's got manners, but boys go missing from his gang, and nobody will say where they went. He don't stick with his mates."

Dunfallon sank slowly back to the bench. "You are eight years old."

Caspar kicked at the dirt. "I might be ten. Petty says boys from the stews come small for their age. I'm a good fighter, though."

Dunfallon's head was filled with a thousand tasks he ought to be seeing to, a dozen other places he could be, and yet, he could not seem to leave the stable.

"You are eight years old," he said again, more softly.

"Mary is eight too," Caspar replied. "O'Keefe tried to give her money, but she wasn't having any of that. Bevins says we need to take special care to walk her home, but we was already seeing to it. We also look after Miss Armstrong. Petty and Bevins help with that." Caspar took a particularly hard kick at the dirt. "O'Keefe has a few girls in his gang. They disappear too. I wish the cat snatchers would grab O'Keefe and toss *him* on a boat."

"But you stick with your mates so you are safe from O'Keefe. What else have you learned from Mr. Dingle, Caspar? Jewel and I are curious."

The boy prosed on, about cat snatchers and kittens, West Bart's, and goats. Sticking with your mates, listening to your ma, washing your paws before a meal, keeping track of the streets so you didn't get lost, and always finding the way home. He chattered as happy boys were meant to chatter, while Dunfallon, who was not a happy boy, listened.

"Would you like some shortbread?" he asked when Caspar paused between diatribes.

"Is it Mrs. Mac's?"

"Yes. Freely given to me to ensure my continuing good behavior." Dunfallon produced the bag and passed over a piece.

"Do all curates talk like you?"

"I thought we had established that I am not a curate."

"So what are you?"

Dunfallon took a piece of shortbread as well. "I thought I was a duke."

"A bleedin' duke? Cor. No wonder you talk so toplofty. And Mr. Mac taught you how to talk, dint he? Does Miss Emmie know you'm a duke?"

"She does. So does Mr. MacAlpin. He was my tutor, long years ago."

Caspar munched his treat. "Is it fine being Yer Grace? Miss Emmie's brother is a lord, but she don't care for him much."

No, it was not fine—yet—but it could be. "A peer can be a lonely fellow," Dunfallon said. "Everybody pretends to be your friend, and it's hard to tell who your mates really are."

"Do dukes allus go around with cats stuffed in their coats?"

Would this child never run out of questions? Dunfallon hoped not. "In the normal course, a cat is not part of ducal sartorial splendor, but I suspect successful authors of children's tales are permitted the occasional feline fashion accessory."

Lucky fellows, those authors. Jewel was a warm, rumbling weight over Dunfallon's heart, and the shortbread was as wonderful as ever.

Though who were his mates? Did he have any mates? Who did he *want* for his mates? Lord Bellefonte was a good friend, but as for *mates...?*

The image of Emmie dozing against Dr. Johnson's life story came to mind.

Bevins and Petty, a two-man court of inquiry.

Wee Mary, demanding her stories and deserving every one of them. Ralph, a young fellow in want of confidence who nonetheless knew who his mates were.

"I am a duke, Caspar, but I am also Christopher Dingle. I used that name to publish my book so nobody would know I'd written the stories."

"Izzat like you have a gang name?"

"Something like it."

"God's bodkin, you be a duke *and* you be our own Mr. Dingle. You should tell Miss Emmie you wrote those stories. She'll fall pure in love with you, and it won't matter you're a duke. She don't like lords, but she'd make an exception for you."

"Have another piece of shortbread," Dunfallon said, shoving the whole parcel at Caspar and getting to his feet. "In fact, keep it, or share it with the goats."

"I'm not giving Mrs. Mac's shortbread to no goats. You still have a cat in your coat, sir."

"Where she apparently thinks she belongs. Caspar, if you were to write a story, one worthy of Mr. Dingle and worthy of our friends at West Bart's Lending, what adventure would you send the kittens on?"

Caspar popped another piece of shortbread into his mouth and studied the goats, who chewed their cud as if they, too, were enjoying some shortbread. The pony and Mac's old horse peered at Caspar through the slats of their stall as if also awaiting his opinion.

"I dunno about adventures, but I like the map game," Caspar said. "The map game can help the kittens find their way home, and you can dedicate the story to West Bart's Lending."

Dunfallon considered the suggestion and caught a tantalizing whiff of literary possibilities. He tousled Caspar's hair—how often had MacAlpin tousled Lord Tertius's hair?—and took his leave.

He was not in a hurry, for once. He had a tale to spin, and the story had to be not simply good, it had to be worthy of Dunfallon's mates.

CHAPTER EIGHT

"Ambrose." Emmie set down Mr. Johnson's Scottish travelogue with a *thump*. "My lord, rather. Welcome to West Bart's Lending." She bobbed a shallow curtsey, which earned her a stiff bow in response.

"Happy Christmas," she added grudgingly. Happy Christmas Eve, more accurately, and to be absolutely punctilious, not all that happy, after all.

The older-sister part of Emmie assessed Ambrose's health, mood, and attire, while another part of her resented him with unseemly intensity for intruding on her sanctuary now of all times. She had parted from her intended three days ago and had not heard from Dunfallon since. Nor had she sent him any cheery little note signaling a return to former good relations.

Her reticence was based on instinct rather than reason. Yes, a duke could be too busy running his duchy to write children's stories, but before he'd been a duke, Dunfallon had been Christopher Dingle. Emmie knew what she owed the duke as a prospective spouse —respect, affection, loyalty. She was less clear about what she owed Mr. Dingle, or what a duke would owe her.

Ambrose did not look particularly pleased to grace West Bart's

Lending with his lordly presence, though he was the pattern card of masculine elegance.

And a small, unignorable part of Emmie rejoiced simply to see her only sibling looking so fine.

"Who's he?" Mary asked, fists on her skinny hips in a manner that presaged forcible ejection of unwanted intruders.

"This is my brother," Emmie said, slipping a hand through Ambrose's arm. "Miss Mary Smith, may I make known to you Ambrose, Viscount Threadham, late of Kent. His lordship is in Town for the holidays. My lord, Miss Mary Smith."

Mary popped a curtsey that would not have been out of place in the boxing ring. Chin barely tipped, hands still planted on her hips. "Now you bow," she said. "Miss Emmie introduced you to me first, because I'm the lady and you be the gent. That's the rule. Now you bow."

Bevins and Petty had roused themselves from their early-midafternoon naps, and Ralph had paused after his seventh pass down the only banister not festooned with ribbons.

Ambrose, to Emmie's shock, offered Mary a proper bow. "Threadham, at your service. Delighted to make your acquaintance, Miss Smith."

"You can call me Mary, but I'll beat yer arse if you get fresh. Caspar showed me where to kick a fellow what gets fresh."

Ambrose's dark eyebrows rose to celestial heights. "You may be assured of my best behavior."

Some of Mary's pugnacity faded. "Will you read us a story? Mr. Dunn reads to us, and he's better at that than even Miss Emmie, but he doesn't come every day. Miss Emmie is very good at readin' stories. I can read too—some."

Drat the child for mentioning Dunfallon, whom Emmie had half hoped to see lugging the day's usual buckets of coal.

"Mary, we've had our story for today. Perhaps you'd remind Ralph not to slide down the banister for me?"

"Ralph! Stop polishing the banister with your butt. Miss Emmie says."

Aristotle, in the midst of his early-midafternoon contemplation session, opened his eyes and glowered at Mary.

"I weren't polishin' the banister," Ralph yelled back.

"Cease squabblin'," Petty barked. "Decorum in the li-bree so a fella can catch a few winks!"

A few months ago, even a few weeks ago, Emmie might have been embarrassed by these displays of informality, but recent days had shifted her perspective. West Bart's Lending was her refuge, and also her castle, more than strong enough to endure raised voices and unruly children.

Ambrose appeared to study the portraits ringing the mezzanine or perhaps the mistletoe that hung beneath them.

"Are you preparing for a journey to Scotland?" he asked.

"Scotland?" Home to the Dukes of Dunfallon since antiquity had acquired its first mist?

Ambrose nodded at Mr. Johnson's travelogue.

"No, of course not. I was just... reshelving the prodigals. Patrons browse, and the books end up wandering, or being wandered. What brings you here, Ambrose?"

"You do, or rather, Aunt's suggestion that I would find you here does. Is there someplace we might talk, Emmie?"

She was in no mood for a lecture from her baby brother about her proper place being in Kent—for *another* lecture. She was also in no mood to be further harangued about the impropriety of her attachment to the library, and she was in no mood *whatsoever* to explain her situation with Dunfallon to his lordship.

"Emmie? Are you well?"

"In the very pink." That had sounded mulish, and Ambrose, whatever his failings, had been a noticing sort of little brother.

"You look as if the dog chewed your copy of *Cecilia* again."

Well, in a manner of speaking... "I enjoy roaring good health. I can offer you tea in my office."

"Thank you."

She'd expected a demurral, if not a protest, but in the past two years, Ambrose had apparently learned some true self-possession to go with his lordly pretensions—and his excellent taste in tailoring.

"The lady goes up the steps first," Mary called, "so you can catch her if she falls on her bum."

"Hush, child," Petty rejoined, though he was smiling.

"That girl has a fixation," Ambrose muttered.

"On manners," Emmie said. "A fine subject for a young lady's focus."

Ambrose let her have the last word, which only increased Emmie's sense of unease. As a boy, he'd battled fiercely—if for the most part fairly—for the final say on any topic.

He's growing up. Emmie considered that complicated thought and revised her conclusion. *He has grown up.* While she'd been dusting biographies and buttering bread, Ambrose had become Lord Threadham in truth.

She could doubtless respect his lordship, but she missed the mischievous, affectionate little brother whom she'd actually liked. Not only was he lost forever, he'd grown a good six inches taller than she, though he wasn't quite as tall as Dunfallon.

Why are the holidays always so hard, and when will I hear from my intended? "In here," she said, pushing open the door to her office. The room bore the aroma of greenery, and that, too, made her think of Dunfallon.

Whom she also missed, drat him.

"Books," Ambrose said, turning a slow circle. "Why am I not surprised?"

"Because West Bart's is a lending library?"

"If I say spinsterhood does not agree with you, you will figuratively kick me in a location Miss Smith would approve of, but, Emmie, I note the books because this is *your* office. Were your office in a shipping warehouse, a convent, or a gaming hell, you would fill the space with books."

Emmie took the kettle from its stand and set it on the parlor stove. "Please have a seat, and I apologize for my shabby manners. You have ambushed me, Ambrose. I thought we might run into each other in the park or at some musicale. I did not expect you to brave West Bart's Lending."

He settled on the old sofa, arm resting along the back, legs crossed at the knee. That Ambrose was tall and well turned out came as a shock, but that he had become *elegant*... How had that happened without her being aware of it?

Without her playing any role in his transformation?

Though she knew how. "I was so angry with you," Emmie said quietly. "So *disappointed* in you." The word brought to mind Dunfallon's assurance that spouses occasionally disappointed each other. But then, Dunfallon was never far from Emmie's thoughts. She had the nagging sense that she'd wronged him by insisting on more stories and an equally nagging sense that for him to refuse to write them was also wrong.

"You are as direct as ever," Ambrose said. "I've missed that. You never let me get away with being the indulged heir and only son."

"Somebody had to prevent you from becoming an ogre."

He smiled slightly, a ghost of his old boyish grin and even more charming. "Or a troll. You had very little patience with trolls. How are you, Emmie?"

The kettle whistled, so she gained a small respite preparing the tray and fetching milk from the window box. When Ambrose ought to have prattled on about the weather, the autumn house parties, or Aunt's choral group, he remained silent.

"I am better," Emmie said, setting the tray on the low table and taking a seat on the sofa. "I needed time, privacy, and some good books after my debacle with Lord Hercules. Aunt saw to it that I had all three, and now I am back on my mettle. Now tell me, *how are you*?"

"You relieve my mind. I am contrite."

"Did you drop Papa's prized Turkish lodestone down the wishing well again?"

"Old business, and you cannot fault my reasoning. If tuppence brought luck, then tossing in an item valued in antiquity should have brought an avalanche of good fortune. Besides, I apologized, and I retrieved Papa's treasure."

"After I told you to go fishing with an iron lure."

"I retrieved the lodestone, and the next harvest was quite good."

They shared a sibling smirk, and Emmie was abruptly pleased to see her brother. The situation with Dunfallon might be irreparable, but cordial relations with Ambrose would be no small holiday boon.

"You were not at Lady Bellefonte's holiday open house," Ambrose said, his expression becoming once again serious. "I had hoped to find you there."

"I sent regrets." Emmie checked the strength of the tea. She rearranged the linen table napkins stacked on the side of the tray. She set out two cups on saucers. "I don't suppose you ran into His Grace of Dunfallon at Lady Bellefonte's?"

"I did not. He was kept away by the press of business, apparently, but I did make the acquaintance of a Miss Peasegill. Interesting woman. She was the only one not making frequent passes beneath a kissing bough. We argued about the mistletoe tradition, and... Well, she put me in mind of you. I did not come here to talk about her or Scottish dukes or boyish pranks."

Emmie poured out two cups of steaming tea and passed one to Ambrose. "What are we to discuss?"

He took a sip of his tea, then set down the cup and saucer, and rose. "I owe you an apology."

Emmie had longed to hear those words, had written one letter after another—all unsent—explaining why Ambrose should offer them to her. His long-awaited apology was of curiously little comfort.

"Apology accepted. How long will you be in Town?"

He went to the window, which looked down on a humble alley

made slightly less disreputable by the light snow dusting everything in white.

"Don't be like that, Emmie. You are the most stubborn woman I know. Don't accept an apology while holding on to your grudge. I was wrong. I behaved very badly, but..."

"But Hercules was so convincing," Emmie said, "and he said enough true things about me—I *am* contrary, I *am* particular, my head *is* full of bookish notions—that you believed his falsehoods as well."

Ambrose sent her a disgruntled glance over his shoulder. "And I did not believe *you* when you stated the situation plainly. Hercules painted himself as the wronged party, the gallant wooer treated cruelly. He even suggested I might try to change your mind."

"A convincing touch, I'm sure, and you apparently declined to take on that challenge."

Ambrose returned to the sofa. "There is no changing your mind, Emmie. Gibraltar is a trifling lump of wet putty compared to your determination once you've dug in your heels."

"While you are the soul of amiable reason at all times?"

He took another sip of tea. "Valid point, but I am here now, and I apologize for my disloyalty. I served you an ill turn when you most needed a sibling's support, and I am deeply sorry for that. I should have listened to you, should have believed that you were being honest with me."

"What changed your mind? You and Hercules were thick as thieves at one point."

"Your tea will get cold."

"The better to dash it in your face when you attempt to prevaricate, Brose."

"Never make empty threats," Ambrose murmured. "You taught me that. Well, you use the word 'thief,' and as it happens, the term applies to dear Hercules. I'd heard rumors at the club, but clubs abound with rumors. Hercules married well, and other bachelors and younger sons found that vexing."

"What sort of rumors?"

"That he cheats at cards." Ambrose's tone expressed profound distaste. "That one doesn't trust him with the valuables at the odd house party. That his wife will hire only older, unattractive maids who prefer to work in pairs when his lordship is in residence. One whisper followed another, and still I thought it all so much idle talk, until he stole from me."

"He stole from us both, Ambrose." Emmie put the words gently, though she was entitled to remind her brother of the facts.

"I cannot call him out, Emmie, but I've considered issuing the challenge anyway."

"Fortunately, you remembered that I would thrash you within an inch of your title for such foolishness. Tell me how he stole from you."

"I invited him down to Kent between house parties, and when he left, I could not find your first edition of Christopher Dingle's *Stories for Young Children*. I wanted to send some of your library to you, if you were determined to bide with Aunt. I found, instead, a second edition. The housekeeper had seen his lordship paging through your more valuable copy. Upon inspection, Hercules had also helped himself to two other first editions and a few curios."

"Mrs. Burney's *Evelina* and Mrs. Radcliffe's *The Female Advocate*. I'd bragged to him about owning both, as well as the Dingle. *Evelina* is signed by the authoress."

"I was aware of that. I got myself invited to the house party Hercules was attending after his stay with me in Kent. I wandered into his lordship's rooms—purely by mistake, of course—and rifled his luggage, also by mistake. I traded the stolen books for the cheaper editions Hercules had left in Kent. I brought your first editions with me to Town and will convey them to you for safekeeping."

Good heavens. Ambrose had become... calculating. Dashing, even.

"Hercules must be desperate if he's stealing from a friend," Emmie said, feeling an unwanted twinge of pity for such a creature, and for Ambrose, who'd been taken in by Hercules's nonsense. "I truly, truly had a narrow escape."

"Hercules and I are not speaking—ever again—and he was not my friend. I should have listened to you, Emmie. I can only blame youthful stupidity and an excess of masculine pride."

"You were a dunderhead, Ambrose. I am not in the habit of serving falsehoods to those I love most dearly." She offered this mild scold because Ambrose seemed to expect it.

Even if Emmie had been inclined to gloat, some inchoate insight dissuaded her from indulging in that pleasure. She had been taken in by Lord Hercules, too, of course, and to as great a degree as her brother had, if not greater.

"Am I forgiven?" Ambrose asked, rising.

Emmie got to her feet, as well because the sounds of some commotion were coming from beyond the door. Mary and Ralph getting into yet another holiday scrap, or maybe the extra order of gingerbread Emmie had put in at the chop shop had arrived.

"You are forgiven," she said, "but I fear I must excuse myself. I don't suppose you can be persuaded to butter some gingerbread?"

"Am I permitted to sample the gingerbread once I've buttered it?"

"Yes," Emmie said, grabbing her brother in a hug. "You were good to come here, Brose. You are right that I am stubborn, though I prefer to think of myself as determined. Hercules made a fool of me, so don't feel too badly that he did the same to you."

Ambrose hugged her back, a good, solid squeeze. "I heard rumors at Bellefonte's do that Hercules is removing to the Continent. Some peer or other has lit a fire under Hercules's creditors and bought up some of his markers. Nobody will say who has performed this public service. Lady Hercules will not accompany her spouse. She's with child and unequal to a winter crossing."

"Good for her." And Emmie was fairly certain she knew who had lit that fire under Hercules's lenders. "I've missed you, Brose." To say that felt very good indeed.

"Missed you too," he said, stepping back as somebody let forth a whoop. "Ye gods and little fishes, what is going on in your library, Emmie?"

"A holiday riot, no doubt. Yuletide has put the younger patrons in high spirits, and we're to have an extra serving of gingerbread in honor of the season." She bustled out the door before those high spirits could turn destructive, just in time to catch Ralph and Mary each making a flying pass down the banister.

"Who the hell is that?" Ambrose muttered, joining Emmie at the top of the steps.

"That is..."

The Duke of Dunfallon, in a green cloak reminiscent of Father Christmas, was ordering a half-dozen footmen about as they set out parcels and boxes and placed a three-foot-high decorated fir tree on the central reading table. "That is an invading army intent on decking the halls. Though I haven't a clue who the white cat is, but she looks very sweet perched on His Grace's shoulder."

The footmen brought in a punchbowl of steaming cider, the spicy scent filling the whole library. Parcels wrapped in red and green cloth were arranged by the tree, and as Aristotle came to attention on the mantel, a veritable feast was laid out between the biographies and the travelogues.

"Emmie," Ambrose said quietly, "are you crying?"

"Of course not." She blinked madly and waved to Dunfallon. "I am not crying, and that is not the Duke of Dunfallon. That is Christopher Dingle himself, and I really must go wish him Happy Christmas."

Emmie stood at the top of the steps attired in the red and green Dunfallon had thought so fetching, a handsome fellow beside her. The real Mr. Dunn, perhaps, and Dunfallon detested him on sight. The man was too exquisitely attired to be a curate and standing entirely too close to the next Duchess of Dunfallon.

"Shall we bring in the rest of the parcels, Your Grace?" the head footman asked.

"You shall, and the corner pub has meat pies and rum punch for the lot of you, including John Coachman and the grooms."

The footman bowed and scurried off, calling to his liveried brethren.

Emmie regarded Dunfallon solemnly, then said something to the handsome blighter and came down from the mezzanine. As she approached Dunfallon, he could see that her lovely green eyes were shiny.

"Did that overdressed popinjay make you cry?" Dunfallon asked, setting Jewel down a safe distance from the Christmas roast. "Something has upset you, Emmie. Tell me what it is, and I'll—"

She launched herself at him and wrapped him in a hug. "You banished the troll. Thank you."

She bore the same brisk, beguiling lemon verbena scent as always, no hint of holiday spirits about her person.

"Emmie, West Bart's Lending would never allow a troll to pass through its doors. Do you refer to a fairy tale?" He held her gently, knowing only that she was upset, and he must restore her good spirits.

"I do, Your Grace. I refer to a fairy tale with a happy ending. We need to talk."

"My love, we must do much more than merely—"

"Will you read us a story?" Mary's strident question cut through the hubbub of chattering children, nattering elders, and Mrs. Oldbach—where had *she* come from?—arguing with two of her library committee members over the placement of the punchbowl.

MacAlpin and his lady arrived at that moment, Caspar swaggering before them like the library's self-appointed majordomo.

"Mary," Emmie said, easing from Dunfallon's arms, "we've had our story for the day. You must stop pestering every passing gentleman to read us a story."

"I pester ladies too," Mary said, chin dipping. "Mr. Dunn said I was the best page turner he ever had. That is a pretty white cat."

The white cat was having a sniff around the hearth while Aristotle watched from above.

"You could read for yourself," Ralph bellowed, "if you'd ever study your letters. I can write me name, and Caspar is almost as good a reader as Miss Emmie. But you be too stubborn and contrary to learn your letters, Mary Smith."

Mary's chin began to quiver, and Dunfallon learned the true meaning of panic. He snatched the girl up and perched her on his hip.

"I have, as it happens, brought a story along with me today. It's a holiday present for our Miss Armstrong from Mr. Christopher Dingle. I also brought the very Jewel herself who inspired Mr. Dingle's stories."

"Mr. Dingle wrote a new story?" Emmie asked. "For me?"

Oh, calamities and catastrophes, she looked ready to cry again. Dunfallon set Mary down within snitching range of a plate of buttered gingerbread.

"Wash your paws, children," he said, doing his best to imitate Emmie's sternest tones. "Then we will feast, and then we will—"

"Am I too late for gingerbread?" The Earl of Bellefonte sauntered in from the foyer, a small girl clinging to his back and a little boy holding his hand. "I heard a rumor stories and gingerbread were to be had for one and all at West Bart's Lending. I can smell the gingerbread, so don't try to hide it from me."

His countess came after him, a little girl dragging her by the hand, a young blond woman at her elbow.

"Next," said the countess, "his lordship will tell you he has been a very good boy. Don't believe him. Miss Armstrong, Your Grace, good day. Children, those are the loveliest cloved oranges I have ever seen."

Petty and Bevins stopped arguing long enough to push to their feet at her ladyship's arrival, and Aristotle squinted at her sagaciously from the mantel.

The popinjay chose then to stroll down from the mezzanine, and Dunfallon was tempted to tell the lot of them that the library was closed for the next thirty minutes in order that he have time to mend his fences with Emmie. Also to read his story to her in private to learn what she thought of his rough draft.

Though thirty minutes wouldn't be nearly long enough for the sort of fence mending he had in mind.

"We should eat before the food gets cold," her ladyship said. "Lord Threadham, a pleasure to see you. Nicholas, do not set a bad example for the children, or I shall be wroth with you."

"Wouldn't think of it, lovey."

Threadham? Dunfallon leaned close to Emmie. "Your brother is here?"

She nodded. "He apologized. We are in charity with one another, and I am dying to hear your new story, but we must also find some time to *talk*, Your Grace."

Dunfallon certainly wanted to talk with Emmie—talk too. "I am dying to know what you think of Mr. Dingle's latest tale. Caspar helped, but I'm out of practice, and penning years of business correspondence doesn't exactly hone one's talent for feline fables."

"Are we planning to do justice to all this lovely food?" Lord Belle-fonte asked. "Or shall we stand around goggling at one another and whispering beneath the mistletoe?"

Emmie swept over to the earl and smacked the giant paw holding a slice of gingerbread. "Don't talk with your mouth full, my lord, and he who sets a bad example must say the blessing."

Bellefonte smiled. "Lovey, I think Miss Emmie likes me. She speaks to me in the same adoring tones I used to hear from you, once upon a time."

"Is he drunk?" Threadham muttered.

"He's in love," Dunfallon replied. "Let's find seats, shall we?"

The meal was merry and loud. Bevins and Petty flirted outrageously with Mrs. Oldbach and her committee members, and Aristotle and Jewel patrolled beneath the table. Bellefonte's brood started a game of hide-and-seek with Caspar, Ralph, Mary, and the other children, and a great quantity of food disappeared.

When the footmen came tottering back from their meal at the pub, Emmie gathered the children around the hearth, and Lord Threadham suggested they join in a song. He chose the ballad of Good King Wenceslas, which boasted at least seventeen verses, and Mrs. Oldbach and Petty knew them all.

As did the footmen, who were in very good voice.

Dunfallon enjoyed every verse, because each one gave him more moments to behold his beloved and to fashion the speech she was owed. She had been right—he suspected Emmie was usually right—and they *would* talk.

"Now we get a story," Mary announced. "Mr. Dunn said."

"He's not really Mr. Dunn," Caspar said. "That was just a nickname. He's really Mr. Dingle, but we have to keep that a secret."

MacAlpin stroked his beard, while Ralph looked confused.

"I have a lot of nicknames," Dunfallon said. "His Grace of Dunfallon is another, Earl of Angelsmere is another. Viscount Dingle is in the pile somewhere, and there are a few baronies as well."

"You're a nob?" Ralph asked.

Emmie would expect him to deal honestly with her patrons. "'Fraid so."

"So am I," Bellefonte said, "but I can't write stories like *he* can. I do have a lovely mare named Buttercup, though. The largest horse you will ever meet, and she can do tricks."

"I'm a viscount," Threadham added. "I hope you won't hold that against me. Miss Emmie is my sister, and she used to read to me."

"I'm just an old lady in the mood for a good story," Mrs. Oldbach said. "Might we commence?"

Mary squirmed beside Mrs. MacAlpin. "Don't you need a page turner?"

Oh, the hope in that question. "Very kind of you to offer, Mary, but this story is so new, it hasn't been printed as part of a proper book. I have only the words on foolscap, and I haven't yet done the sketches."

"When you have this story as a book, I will turn your pages. You have to start with 'once upon a time.'"

Mary enjoyed great confidence in her opinions, but she was sometimes in error. "I will start with the title and dedication. *Under a Mousing Moon* by Mr. Christopher Dingle, dedicated to Miss Emmie of West Bart's Lending, guardian of truth and worker of miracles."

The fidgeting and squirming subsided, and on the mantel, Jewel and Aristotle started up antiphonal purring.

"'Once upon a time,'" Dunfallon began, "'there were four mostly well-behaved kittens named Hammerhead, Mark, Luke, and Jewel...'"

The pages shook slightly in his hand, but by the time he'd reached the part about the kittens wandering the town in search of the merest morsel of food, and the children were calling out directions to the fictitious kittens, he'd hit his stride. Emmie's eyes were shining again—in a good way—and when the kittens found their way home, as they always did, the library reverberated with applause.

The gathering broke up in phases, with the footmen disappearing first, carrying boxes of leftovers. Mrs. Oldbach's contingent departed next, chattering like starlings about West Bart's Lending being the brightest gem in the committee's crown. The pensioners decamped with the ladies, providing escort and flirtation in equal measure.

Lord Bellefonte gathered up his family, though he did murmur something in Emmie's ear before taking his leave of her.

MacAlpin collected his wife, Caspar, Ralph, and Mary, along with the older boys who were so inclined, amid talk of a Christmas Eve map game tournament.

Last to go was Lord Threadham, who looked like a man with a few fraternal warnings on his mind.

"Don't disappoint her, Dunfallon," Threadham said as Emmie moved around the library, blowing out sconces. "She was ill-used once, and I could not call the blighter out because he was a commoner. You are titled, when you bother to recall your nicknames, so watch your step."

"I have already disappointed her," Dunfallon said. "We appear to have weathered my blundering. If you will take your splendid, lordly self off, I will make a proper proposal to my prospective duchess and pay my addresses to Mr. Dingle's intended."

Emmie paused to reshelve a book here and to tidy up a stack of magazines there. She was all of a piece with this stately old library, and yet, she shone like a jewel in her own right too.

Threadham extended a hand. "Welcome to the family, Mr. Dingle."

They shook. Threadham offered a farewell to his sister and promised to call upon her and their aunt Christmas morning.

Emmie waved and blew out the last sconce as Threadham took his leave. "Finally," she said, coming around the biographies to wrap an arm about Dunfallon's middle. "I would like to challenge you to a holiday sofa-measuring contest, sir, but first, I have a few things I need to say to you."

"Let's sit by the fire, shall we? Before you launch into the scolds I abundantly deserve, Emmie, allow me to explain."

She leaned against him, the sweetest holiday gift imaginable. "What utter rot. I was wrong, and you will allow me to make my apologies. Ladies first, Your Grace, or must we have Mary remind you of your manners?"

"I like it better when you call me Mr. Dingle and best when you call me Dane."

"I adore it when you tell me I'm your love. Let's talk."

She led him to the reading chairs before the hearth, while on the mantel, Jewel and Aristotle ever so delicately touched noses.

"Mary will learn her letters now," Emmie said, which seemed a safe enough thing to say while falling in love all over again with a duke who hauled coal, managed Christmas feasts, and wrote gorgeous little stories. "The children—I mean, the kittens—found their way home safely because they knew the map of London, and because they could read the street signs and building markers."

Clever of him, to weave that lesson into the adventure, but then, Mr. Dingle was a very clever fellow. "Mrs. MacAlpin," Emmie went on, "allowed as how she could use a little helper around the house, and I saw Mr. MacAlpin making a bird out of paper for Ralph. Ralph is clever with his hands, and he'll..."

Dunfallon smiled at her. "Yes, my love?"

"I can't think when you do that."

"Smile at you?"

"Call me your love in that purring tone. You are my love too."

His smile faded. "That is the greatest gift I have ever been given, Emmie. You were right, you know, about the stories—about me."

"No," Emmie said, rising and pacing before the hearth. "You will not apologize first, Dunfallon. I will apologize to you. *I did not listen to you.* You said not only that you would not write more stories, but that you *could* not. I *could not* face Society for a time—could not— and nobody but my aunt believed me. You are not some mechanical marvel who can produce stories merely because I adore what you write. You are a busy man, a peer, and I had no business trampling your truth."

One moment, Emmie was pacing with righteous determination. The next, she was perched in Dunfallon's lap, his fingers circling her wrist.

"Is Miss quite through with her diatribe?"

"No. You might have asked me to sit in your lap."

"You might have bestowed the privilege of your presence upon my person, and I hope in future you often will." He kissed her cheek, and when Emmie ought to have scolded him—where did Lady Belle-fonte get her fortitude?—she cuddled against his chest.

"My brother did not listen to me," she said. "I explained to him exactly what had happened with Lord Hercules at the time of that scoundrel's defection, and Ambrose could not credit my version of events. I could not *make* him listen, and I never want you to feel the misery that I did when my only sibling turned a deaf ear on my misfortune. I will tell you when you are wrong, Dunfallon, but I will also listen to you. Truly listen, not simply hoard up ammunition for my next volley in the argument. We can both be right, and we can both be wrong, all at the same time. You should write more stories—I was right about that—and I should have respected your demurral."

Dunfallon's fingers stroked Emmie's hair from her temple to her nape, a deliciously soothing touch. "You propose a sound bargain. I promise you both honesty and kindness, and that means listening to each other even when we are disappointed or dismayed, but it also means we don't lie to ourselves."

"You could never—"

"I did, or I failed to see what you were trying to tell me. Caspar sorted me out. Caspar and MacAlpin. I was becoming my father, absorbed with the honors and duties of my station, and those honors and duties are important. The stories, as you so easily grasped, are important too. It's not one or the other, I can do both, with proper inspiration and assistance. Do you know why Mary doesn't learn her letters?"

"Because she's a prodigy with numbers?"

"Because her mother cannot read. Mary has it in her stubborn little head that if she learns to read, she will make her mother feel stupid, and her mother—a streetwalker overly fond of gin, to hear Caspar tell it—is all she has. Mary also thinks that once she learns her letters, nobody will ever read her a story again."

"But Caspar reads fairly well, and he's..."

"He's off to greater ventures. Nobody is reading to him, or so Mary thinks. Caspar explained it to me."

Emmie wanted to catch up with the MacAlpins, take Mary by the hand, and explain to the child that nobody is too old to enjoy a story hour. Not too old, not too well-read, not too important.

She also wanted to close her eyes and snuggle closer to Dunfallon, so she did. "Dane?"

"Hmm?"

"When I am an old and crotchety duchess sitting on too many committees and fond of too many cats, will you still read to me?"

He kissed her cheek. "Of course, and you will read to me, and we will argue over our stories and over reform bills and gingerbread, but we will also listen to each other."

"You may have all the gingerbread you please. What else did Caspar say?"

Dunfallon's caresses weren't putting Emmie to sleep so much as they were easing away all the worries she'd stored up over the past few days and past few years. She was pleasantly aware of him in a physical sense, but more significantly, she felt restored to emotional closeness with him.

Honesty could do that. Honesty and love.

"Caspar said a great deal. He reminded me that stories have the power to fortify us against temptation, against bad decisions, against loneliness. He explained to me—not in so many words—that Mr. Dingle had done more to protect him against turning to a life of crime than all the sermons or charitable committees in London have done."

"Gingerbread and cider played a hand in keeping him safe thus far too, Dane."

"As did the physical refuge of West Bart's Lending and the friends he made here. I wrote those stories to fortify myself, Emmie. I had lost sight of what they might do for other people. I saw in myself only the duke my father intended me to become, and I had lost sight of Mr. Dingle entirely."

"Are you quite through with your apology, sir?"

He hugged her. "Yes. Happy Christmas, Emmie. Did you know that emeralds are worth more than rubies?"

"What are you going on about?"

"I am expounding on my heart's greatest treasure. Will you marry me?"

She kissed his cheek. "Happy Christmas, Dane. Yes, I will marry you. Have you more story ideas?"

"As it happens, I do, and I'm sure you do, too, but might we discuss them later?"

A lovely glow spread through her. "You are inclined to measure my office sofa with me?"

"Something like that."

"I thought you'd never ask."

She led him between the bookshelves and up the steps, past all the kissing boughs and portraits, past the plays and periodicals, to her cozy office, where His Grace of Dunfallon found that—contrary to his earlier supposition—Miss Emmie's office sofa was a perfect place to celebrate a holiday engagement.

And they lived happily—also noisily, lovingly, and honestly—ever after!

TO MY DEAR READERS

Oh, dontcha just love a holiday happily ever after? I wrote this story in part because I delight in seasonal romances, and also because I delight in books. I well remember that day in second grade when my teacher turned the class loose in the school library for the first time. Aladdin's Cave of Wonders paled for me by comparison.

My local public library figured prominently in my middle-school years in particular, and started me on a path that ultimately led to a degree in music history and many lucrative and enjoyable hours at the piano.

If you want some interesting reading, try binging the lives of the composers. Yikes!

As you think about your TBR pile this holiday season, please spare a thought for your local library too. Most of them have donation buttons on their web sites, and they enrich our communities with so much more than "just" books.

But speaking of books... I have a few more on the way. *The Lord Julian Mysteries* launched in August with **A Gentleman Fallen on Hard Times**. Book two, **A Gentleman of Dubious Reputation**, is available now from my **web store** and in **print**, and will launch on the **retail sites** on November Nov. 3. Book Three, ***A Gentleman in Challenging Circumstances***, will be available from the **web store** on Oct. 24, and launch on the **retail sites** Dec. 5.

And if you haven't crossed paths with his lordship, I've included an excerpt from ***A Gentleman of Dubious Reputation*** below.

But what about the romances, you ask? No worries! ***Miss Dramatic***, our next Mischief in Mayfair title, will be available from the **web store** on Nov. 14, and launch on the **retail sites** Nov. 28. Excerpt below.

Am I going to have a busy end to my year or what? Wheee!

Happy reading!

Grace Burrowes

Read on for excerpts from ***A Gentleman of Dubious Reputation***, and ***Miss Dramatic!***

A GENTLEMAN OF DUBIOUS
REPUTATION—EXCERPT

Chapter One

On my lengthy list of reasons for avoiding the Caldicott family seat, Harry's ghost took top honors. My oldest sibling, Arthur (still extant), came third, and Lady Clarissa Valmond (lively indeed) occupied the spot between them.

Harry haunted me even when I wasn't at Caldicott Hall, appearing in my daydreams and nightmares. Like the good brother he'd been, he did not stand on ceremony in death any more than he had in life. I'd nonetheless been relieved to quit the Hall months ago to finish recuperating at my London town house, though I'd yet to achieve a full return to health.

After parting ways with the military following Waterloo, I'd come home from the Continent in poor health. My eyes still objected to prolonged bright light, my stamina wasn't what it had been on campaign, my hair was nearly white, and my memory...

My memory had been a problem before I'd bought my commission.

And yet, I knew every tree of the lime alley that led to the Hall, forty-eight in all, though two were relative saplings, having been planted in my great-grandfather's day. The other forty-six were nearly four hundred years old, but for a few new recruits necessitated by lightning strikes, Channel storms, and other random misfortunes.

Atlas, my horse, knew the path to the Hall as well as I did and picked up his pace as we turned through the ornate main gate.

"You would not be so eager to complete this journey if His Grace had summoned you," I muttered.

Arthur had signed his summons with an *A*, meaning as a brother, not as the Duke of Waltham and head of the family. He was six years my senior and possessed of worlds more consequence, not merely by virtue of his title. Arthur carried the dignity of his station as naturally as a gunnery sergeant carried a spare powder bag.

He had been born to be a duke, just as Harry had been a natural fit with the role of charming spare. Our father had assured me many times that my lot in life was to be the despair of his waning years.

Atlas marched on, his horsey imagination doubtless filled with visions of lush summer grass and long naps in sunny paddocks. Harry and I had raced up the lime alley more times than I could count, on foot and on horseback and, once when slightly inebriated, running backward.

In earliest boyhood, I'd routinely lost. Harry had had two years on me, and for much of my youth, that had meant size and reach. Then Harry attained his full height, and I kept growing. Had he lived to be an old, old man, I'd have delighted in reminding him that I was the tallest Caldicott son, having an inch on Harry and a half inch on Arthur.

What I would not give to gloat over that inch to him in person.

Harry had been taken captive by the French, and I had followed him into French hands, thinking the two of us could somehow win free where one could not. I am not the smartest of the Caldicotts, clearly. Harry had expired without yielding any information to his captors, while my experience as a prisoner was complicated by...

Many factors.

I'd survived and escaped, and I'd do the same again if need be, but now that I was back in Merry Olde, public opinion castigated me for having the effrontery to outlive my brother. At least one faction of the military gossip brigade concluded that I'd bought my life through dishonorable means—betraying my commission—though the military itself had cleared me of such allegations.

Arthur had welcomed me home with the reserve of a duke. Not until we had been private had he informed me that acts of self-harm on my part would reflect poorly on the family honor. I was not to indulge in foolish histrionics simply because I'd been labeled a traitor, much less because I could barely see, my memory was worse than ever, and I never slept more than two hours at a stretch.

Petty annoyances were no justification for imbecilic stunts, according to Arthur. He'd delivered that scold with characteristic sternness, though I'd never wanted so badly to hug him.

One did not presume on ducal dignity. My time among the French had also left me with a peculiar reluctance to be touched. With few exceptions, I kept my hands to myself and hoped others would do likewise concerning my person.

I emerged from the lime alley to behold the Hall, sitting uphill on the opposite bank of William's Creek. That placid stream was named for a multiple-great-grandfather, who'd no doubt played in its shallows as Harry and I had. Aided by juvenile imagination, that waterway had been the English Channel, where we'd defeated the great Spanish Armada; the Thames; the raging North Atlantic; and the South China Sea.

As Atlas clip-clopped over the arched stone bridge, a pang of longing assailed me, for Harry's voice, for his presence, for even his relentless teasing and boasting. Why did Harry have to die? Why had he left camp that night? Why hadn't the French taken my life as they'd taken his?

I'd asked those questions a thousand times, though I posed them now with more sadness than despair.

Caldicott Hall was sometimes referred to as Chatsworth in

miniature, meaning the Hall was merely huge as opposed to gargan-
tuan. Like the Duke of Devonshire's seat up in Derbyshire, the Hall
was built around a central open quadrangle. All four exterior
approaches presented dignified, symmetric façades of golden lime-
stone, with obligatory pilasters and entablatures adding an appear-
ance of staid antiquity.

I drew Atlas to a halt, giving myself a moment to appreciate my
family home and to gather my courage. My mother was off at some
seaside gossip fest, thank the merciful powers, but Harry's ghost was
doubtless in residence, as was my father's. And if that wasn't enough
to give a fellow pause, my godmother, Lady Ophelia Oliphant, had
threatened to follow me to the Hall once she'd tended to some social
obligations.

Atlas rooted at the reins, suggesting a dutiful steed deserved his
bucket of oats sooner rather than later. A slight movement from the
window at the corner of the second floor caught my eye.

"We've been sighted," I muttered, letting the beast shuffle
forward. "The advance guard should be out in less time than it takes
Prinny to down a glass of port."

Half a minute later, a groom jogged up from the direction of the
stable and stood at attention by the gents' mounting block. As Atlas
plodded on, I nearly fell out of the saddle.

A footman coming forth to take charge of my saddlebags would
not have been unusual.

The butler, Cheadle, might have welcomed me home in a fit of
sentimentality, or one of my sisters might have bestirred herself to
greet me if she were calling on Arthur.

Arthur *himself* sauntered out of the house, checked the time on
his watch—which had been Papa's watch—and surveyed the clouds
as if a perfectly benign summer sky required minute inspection. He
was to all appearances the epitome of the reserved country gentleman. Tall, athletic, his wavy dark hair neatly combed, his aquiline
profile the envy of portraitists and sculptors.

To the educated fraternal eye, though, the duke was in the next thing to a panic. His Grace set very great store by decorum. When I had returned from France after escaping from captivity and before the Hundred Days, Arthur had received me in the library and offered me a brandy in Harry's memory.

All quite civilized, though at the time, I'd been barely able to remain upright, my hands had shaken like an old man's, and I'd managed a mere sip of libation. When I'd come home from Waterloo, Arthur had merely greeted me at supper as if I'd been up to Town for a few fittings.

Before my wondering eyes, he came down the terrace steps and joined the groom at the mounting block. I swung from the saddle, taking care to have my balance before I turned loose of Atlas's mane. I'd fallen on my arse a time or two after a hard ride, but I refused to give Arthur the satisfaction of witnessing my humiliation.

"You are a welcome sight, Demming," I said to the towheaded groom as I untied my saddlebags. "Don't bother too much brushing Atlas out. A stop at the water trough, a quick currying, and a shady paddock once he's finished cooling out will be the answer to his prayers. Then he will roll in the first dusty patch he can find."

"Aye, milord," Demming replied. "Does himself get oats for his trouble?"

"A mash tonight wouldn't go amiss, but no oats until tomorrow if there's grass to be had."

"We've plenty of that. Come along, beastie."

Arthur was an accomplished horseman and would not begrudge Atlas good care, but impatience rolled off the ducal person as Demming led Atlas away. Now would come an interrogation. Had my journey been uneventful? How was Lady Ophelia? Was there any particular news from Town, and what did the physicians say about my dodgy eyesight? What exactly had happened at the Makepeace house party, and where were my valet, footman, groom, and coach?

"She's driving me mad," Arthur said, striding off toward the terrace steps. "The damned Valmond woman leaves me no peace, and it's well past time you took a bride."

Order your copy of *A Gentleman of Dubious Reputation* and read on for an excerpt from *Miss Dramatic*!

MISS DRAMATIC—EXCERPT

Chapter One

"Are you two out of your happily married minds?"

Gavin DeWitt did not shout, nor did he pitch the nearest porcelain vase to the hearthstones or lapse into profanity. The acting profession taught a man to control himself before all audiences, as did life in Crosspatch Corners. "The only curse worse than a house party," he went on, "is a hen party, and you propose to gather up every clucking biddy ever to roost at a Mayfair ridotto."

"Remind me again," Lord Phillip Vincent drawled. "What exactly is a ridotto?"

His brother, Trevor, Marquess of Tavistock, lounged with an elbow on the library mantel. "The usual dancing and flirtation. Better food at a ball, better gaming at a ridotto."

"Ah." Phillip had taken to studying the niceties of polite society as Gavin might have applied himself to a Shakespeare soliloquy. "Interesting."

Gavin considered pitching the vase at the marquess, his brother-by-marriage. "*A learned fool is more a fool than an ignorant fool. If* you know polite society so well, Tavistock, then you know this gathering will only end in disaster."

Tavistock merely smiled in that urbane, self-possessed way of his. "In finding you a wife, you mean?"

Lord Phillip rose from the desk. "Stow it, Tavistock. Gloating is bad form even here in the shires. Just because you and I are the happiest of men, delighting in the affections of our darling wives, doesn't mean you should tease DeWitt about his lamentable bachelorhood."

Neither Moliere nor the Bard offered a riposte worthy of that bit of inanity. "I like my bachelorhood very well, thank you, and I intend to enjoy it for some time."

Tavistock and Lord Phillip exchanged a look possible only between men who were both in the early throes of wedded bliss. Tavistock was fair, Lord Phillip dark-haired, but the pair of them were tall and rangy, and they shared a certain resemblance in their features.

And in their patient pitying of Gavin's bachelor state.

"I was like you once," Tavistock said, as if *once* had been ages and ages ago in a land far away, not a mere handful of weeks most of them spent in Crosspatch Corners. "Determined to avoid parson's mousetrap, but I had a reason: My father's example would have put any man off marriage. Phillip was concerned about his past overshadowing his future, which we can also lay at our late father's feet. What's your excuse?"

"Why do I need an excuse to enjoy my freedom? Phillip, you professed the self-same contentment until very recently."

Phillip's smile was sweet, and that hurt worse than Tavistock's smug condescension. "Then I met my Hecate, and mere contentment would no longer do, though I understand your hesitation. Women like Hecate and Amaryllis are rare."

Phillip had been raised in Crosspatch Corners, far from the madding crowd's ignoble strife—and its licentiousness. He was in some regards the most innocent of men, though in his understated, soft-spoken way, also quite shrewd.

"You could not possibly understand why the prospect of a lot of spinsters and meddlers congregating beneath my very nose gives me the collywobbles." Opening night on Drury Lane wouldn't have been half so intimidating. "These are the ladies who make up numbers, who pop up on short notice when more fashionable guests decline an invitation at the last minute. They aren't half so harmless as you might think. You have no idea..."

Phillip and Tavistock were looking at him as if he'd lapsed into Old English.

"You've been off racketing about the shires for two years," Tavistock said. "Doing your Shakespeare impersonation. How could you predict the sort of women Hecate and Amaryllis will favor with an invitation?"

The former Miss Hecate Brompton was not well known to Gavin, but he was better acquainted with his sister Amaryllis than with any other person living upon the earth. He could predict exactly what sort of ladies she'd invite to Berkshire for a few weeks of summer socializing.

Dragons in disguise, basilisks in bonnets, wyverns in white gloves.

"While I was on the stage," Gavin said, "my troupe was occasionally called up on to grace social gatherings."

Phillip squinted at him. "You were hired to entertain in private homes. Juggle for your supper?"

If only the expected entertainments had been limited to juggling. "We enacted selected scenes, delivered famous speeches, and assisted with the amateur theatricals. We were also expected to serve as supporting cast."

"Flirt with the dowagers?" Tavistock pushed away from the mantel. "So you rounded out the dance sets when you weren't mooning about the court of Denmark or preparing to storm Agincourt. What of it?"

Both men regarded Gavin with genuine puzzlement. If he told

them the rest of it, that puzzlement might well turn to disgust or amusement. The situation wanted some thought, some rehearsal. He'd find a way to explain, a way to say what needed to be said without making himself look like the ignorant Yahoo he'd been.

"For the good of all concerned," he said, "the only role I will be playing for next few years is the country squire conscientiously minding his acres right here in Crosspatch Corners. Perhaps after Mama sees Caroline and Diana launched, I will see fit to add a wife to the cast at Twidboro Hall."

"Wife is not a part to be acted," Phillip said, "any more than husband is a role to be put on and taken off. One fears for your understanding, DeWitt."

Better that than fearing for a man's good name.

"You won't run off?" Tavistock asked, ever so casually. "Hecate and Amaryllis have quite warmed to the idea of a mostly-ladies gathering, and if you were to absent yourself, they would be puzzled."

Amaryllis would be hurt, possibly furious. "I won't run off." Appending the word *again* was unnecessary. For the two years Gavin been racketing about the provincial stages, his family hadn't known where to find him, through no direct fault of his.

The indirect fault had been and remained entirely his.

"Splendid." Phillip came around the desk and clapped him on the back. "You will enjoy yourself, and we might even let you do some of that to-be-or-not-to-be business. The guests we're expecting are a bookish lot, and they will doubtless appreciate some rousing speeches from a tall, dark, and brooding Hamlet."

"Not Hamlet," Gavin said, and brooding was doing it a bit brown. "The poor fellow went mad, committed suicide by duel, and left his kingdom ripe for plucking by a foreign invader. I don't suppose you have a copy of the guest list?"

Another shared glance that spoke volumes. "*Got him!*" from Tavistock, and "*I told you he'd come around,*" from Phillip.

Tavistock opened the desk's middle drawer and brandished a

piece of foolscap. "Might not be complete, but these are the ladies who have accepted."

Gavin read down the list, recognized a few names, and allowed himself a gathering sense of relief. Formidable women, but none with a reason to wish him ill. No drunkards or hopeless gamblers, no prattling...

Oh, spite. Oh, hell. His dearest memory, his deepest regret lurked near the bottom of list, gracing the space between Lady Iris Wolverhampton and Miss Zinnia Peasegood.

"You see some familiar names, I trust?" Lord Phillip sounded pleased with himself. "I know you and Mrs. Roberts are cordially acquainted."

"Rose Roberts was at the Nunnsuch house party, wasn't she?" Tavistock asked, overdoing the curious tone by half. "A widow, as I recollect."

"Mrs. Roberts was at Nunnsuch," Gavin replied, passing back the list. "An agreeable, sensible lady."

"And easy on the eyes," Phillip added. "Surely you noticed that part?"

How could Gavin have failed to notice that a woman who'd been luminous eighteen months ago despite her grief had bloomed in the wake of mourning? Hair between auburn and Titian that loved both sunlight and candlelight, a smile to intrigue even a saint—Gavin was not a saint—and silences that could bless or condemn. Then there were her hands, her eyes, the way she caressed the rim of her wine glass when her thoughts wandered...

"Quite pretty," Gavin said. "Also well read, and much enamored of her late spouse, if I'm to believe the Earl of Nunn. I can see why Amaryllis would enjoy her company. Unless you two have any more ambushes to spring upon me, I'm off to see Old Man Deever about a new pair of riding boots."

The bedrock of any successful role was in the details. Which hat would a rake wear to see his mistress? Which would he wear to take supper at his sister's house? The audience noticed those details, even if they didn't realize they noticed.

The mention of riding boots was a such a detail—Gavin was notably fond of his colt, Roland—and apparently convincing.

"My regards to the Deevers," Tavistock said. "Amaryllis and I will expect you and the rest of the family for supper tomorrow evening."

Gavin assayed his best, harmless smile. "Wouldn't miss it for the world."

He knew not to rush his exit and denied himself a moment to tarry in the wings. He cared not one fresh horse dropping how Phillip and Tavistock parsed the conversation.

He knew only that this hen party could foretell his doom, but that he'd risk even his good name if he could once again escort Mrs. Rose Roberts in to dinner.

Order your copy of *Miss Dramatic!*